RANDOM HOUSE

LARGE
PRINT

Nights in Rodanthe

Also by Nicholas Sparks
available from Random House Large Print

A Walk to Remember
The Rescue
A Bend in the Road

NICHOLAS SPARKS

Nights in Rodanthe

R A N D O M  H O U S E
L A R G E   P R I N T

Published in the United States of America by Random House Large Print in association with Warner Books, Inc., New York and simultaneously in Canada by Random House of Canada Limited, Toronto. Distributed by Random House, Inc., New York.

www.randomlargeprint.com

Library of Congress Cataloging-in-Publication Data
Sparks, Nicholas.
Nights in Rodanthe/Nicholas Sparks.
p. cm.
ISBN 0-375-43088-1
1. Rodanthe (N.C.)—Fiction. 2. North Carolina—Fiction. 3. Divorced people—Fiction. 4. Hotelkeepers—Fiction. 5. Storms—Fiction. 6. Large type books.
I. Title.

PS3569.P363 N54 2002b
813'.54—dc21
2002069863

FIRST LARGE PRINT EDITION

This Large Print edition published in accord with the standards of the N.A.V.H.

For Landon, Lexie, and Savannah

Acknowledgments

Nights In Rodanthe, as with all my novels, couldn't have been written without the patience, love, and support of my wife, Cathy. She only gets more beautiful every year.

Since the dedication is to my other three children, I have to acknowledge both Miles and Ryan (who got a dedication in *Message in a Bottle*). I love you guys!

I'd also like to thank Theresa Park and Jamie Raab, my agent and editor respectively. Not only do they both have wonderful instincts, but they never let me slide when it comes to my writing. Though I sometimes grumble about the challenges this presents, the final product is what it is because of those two. If they like the story, odds are that you will, too.

Larry Kirshbaum and Maureen Egen at Warner Books also deserve my thanks. When I go to New York, spending time with them is like visiting with my family. They've made Warner Books a wonderful home for me.

Denise Di Novi, the producer of both *Message in a Bottle* and *A Walk to Remember* is not only skilled at what she does, but someone I trust and respect. She's a good friend, and she deserves my thanks for all she has done—and still does—for me.

Richard Green and Howie Sanders, my agents in Hollywood, are great friends, great people, and great at what they do. Thanks, guys.

Scott Schwimer, my attorney and friend, always watches out for me. Thank you.

In publicity, I have to thank Jennifer Romanello, Emi Battaglia, and Edna Farley; Flag and the rest of the cover design people; Courtenay Valenti and Lorenzo De Bonaventura of Warner Brothers; Hunt Lowry and Ed Gaylord II, of Gaylord Films; Mark Johnson and Lynn Harris of New Line Cinema have all been great to work with. Thanks everyone.

Mandy Moore and Shane West were both wonderful in *A Walk to Remember,* and I appreciate their enthusiasm for the project.

Then there is family (who might get a kick out of seeing their names here): Micah, Christine, Alli and Peyton; Bob, Debbie, Cody and Cole. Mike and Parnell, Henrietta, Charles and Glenara, Duke and Marge, Dianne and John, Monte and Gail, Dan and Sandy, Jack, Carlin, Joe, Elaine and Mark, Michelle and Lemont, Paul, John and Caroline, Tim, Joannie and Papa Paul.

And, of course, how can I forget Paul and Adrienne?

Nights in Rodanthe

One

─◆─

Three years earlier, on a warm November morning in 1999, Adrienne Willis had returned to the Inn and at first glance had thought it unchanged, as if the small Inn were impervious to sun and sand and salted mist. The porch had been freshly painted, and shiny black shutters sandwiched rectangular white-curtained windows on both floors like offset piano keys. The cedar siding was the color of dusty snow. On either side of the building, sea oats waved a greeting, and sand formed a curving dune that changed imperceptibly with each passing day as individual grains shifted from one spot to the next.

With the sun hovering among the clouds, the air had a luminescent quality, as though particles of light were suspended in the haze, and for a moment Adrienne felt she'd traveled back in time. But looking closer, she gradually began to notice changes that cosmetic work couldn't hide: decay at the corners of the windows, lines of rust along the roof, water stains near the gutters. The Inn seemed to be winding down, and though she knew there was nothing she could do to change it, Adrienne remembered closing her eyes, as if to magically blink it back to what it had once been.

Now, standing in the kitchen of her own home a few months into her sixtieth year, Adrienne hung up the phone after speaking with her daughter. She sat at the table, reflecting on that last visit to the Inn, remembering the long weekend she'd once spent there. Despite all that had happened in the years that had passed since then, Adrienne still held tight to the belief that love was the essence of a full and wonderful life.

Outside, rain was falling. Listening to the gentle tapping against the glass, she was thankful for its steady sense of familiarity. Remembering those days always aroused a mixture of emotions in her— something akin to, but not quite, nostalgia. Nostalgia was often romanticized; with these memories, there was no reason to make them any more romantic than they already were. Nor did she share these memories with others. They were hers, and over the years, she'd come to view them as a sort of museum exhibit, one in which she was both the curator and the only patron. And in an odd way, Adrienne had come to believe that she'd learned more in those five days than she had in all the years before or after.

She was alone in the house. Her children were grown, her father had passed away in 1996, and she'd been divorced from Jack for seventeen years now.

Though her sons sometimes urged her to find someone to spend her remaining years with, Adrienne had no desire to do so. It wasn't that she was wary of men; on the contrary, even now she occasionally found her eyes drawn to younger men in the supermarket. Since they were sometimes only a few years older than her own children, she was curious about what they would think if they noticed her staring at them. Would they dismiss her out of hand? Or would they smile back at her, finding her interest charming? She wasn't sure. Nor did she know if it was possible for them to look past the graying hair and wrinkles and see the woman she used to be.

Not that she regretted being older. People nowadays talked incessantly about the glories of youth, but Adrienne had no desire to be young again. Middle-aged, maybe, but not young. True, she missed some things—bounding up the stairs, carrying more than one bag of groceries at a time, or having the energy to keep up with the grandchildren as they raced around the yard—but she'd gladly exchange them for the experiences she'd had, and those came only with age. It was the fact that she could look back on life and realize she wouldn't have changed much at all that made sleep come easy these days.

Besides, youth had its problems. Not only did she remember them from her own life, but she'd watched her children as they'd struggled through the angst of adolescence and the uncertainty and chaos of their early twenties. Even though two of them were now in their thirties and one was almost there, she sometimes wondered when motherhood would become less than a full-time job.

Matt was thirty-two, Amanda was thirty-one, and Dan had just turned twenty-nine. They'd all gone to college, and she was proud of that, since there'd been a time when she wasn't sure any of them would. They were honest, kind, and self-sufficient, and for the most part, that was all she'd ever wanted for them. Matt worked as an accountant, Dan was the sportscaster on the evening news out in Greenville, and both were married with families of their own. When they'd come over for Thanksgiving, she remembered sitting off to the side and watching them scurry after their children, feeling strangely satisfied at the way everything had turned out for her sons.

As always, things were a little more complicated for her daughter.

The kids were fourteen, thirteen, and eleven when Jack moved out of the house, and each child had dealt with the divorce in a different way. Matt and Dan took out their aggression on the athletic fields and by occasionally acting up in school, but Amanda had been the most affected. As the middle child sandwiched between brothers, she'd always been the most sensitive, and as a teenager, she'd needed her father in the house, if only to distract from the worried stares of her mother. She began dressing in what

Adrienne considered rags, hung with a crowd that stayed out late, and swore she was deeply in love with at least a dozen different boys over the next couple of years. After school, she spent hours in her room listening to music that made the walls vibrate, ignoring her mother's calls for dinner. There were periods when she would barely speak to her mother or brothers for days.

It took a few years, but Amanda had eventually found her way, settling into a life that felt strangely similar to what Adrienne once had. She met Brent in college, and they married after graduation and had two kids in the first few years of marriage. Like many young couples, they struggled financially, but Brent was prudent in a way that Jack never had been. As soon as their first child was born, he bought life insurance as a precaution, though neither expected that they would need it for a long, long time.

They were wrong.

Brent had been gone for eight months

now, the victim of a virulent strain of testicular cancer. Adrienne had watched Amanda sink into a deep depression, and yesterday afternoon, when she dropped off the grandchildren after spending some time with them, she found the drapes at their house drawn, the porch light still on, and Amanda sitting in the living room in her bathrobe with the same vacant expression she'd worn on the day of the funeral.

It was then, while standing in Amanda's living room, that Adrienne knew it was time to tell her daughter about the past.

Fourteen years. That's how long it had been.

In all those years, Adrienne had told only one person about what had happened, but her father had died with the secret, unable to tell anyone even if he'd wanted to.

Her mother had passed away when

Adrienne was thirty-five, and though they'd had a good relationship, she'd always been closest to her father. He was, she still thought, one of two men who'd ever really understood her, and she missed him now that he was gone. His life had been typical of so many of his generation. Having learned a trade instead of going to college, he'd spent forty years in a furniture manufacturing plant working for an hourly wage that increased by pennies each January. He wore fedoras even during the warm summer months, carried his lunch in a box with squeaky hinges, and left the house promptly at six forty-five every morning to walk the mile and a half to work.

In the evenings after dinner, he wore a cardigan sweater and long-sleeved shirts. His wrinkled pants lent a disheveled air to his appearance that grew more pronounced as the years wore on, especially after the passing of his wife. He liked to sit in the easy chair with the yellow lamp glowing beside him, reading genre westerns and books about World War II. In the final years before his strokes, his old-fashioned spectacles, bushy eyebrows, and deeply lined face made him look more like a retired college professor than the blue-collar worker he had been.

There was a peacefulness about her father that she'd always yearned to emulate. He would have made a good priest or minister, she'd often thought, and people who met him for the first time usually walked away with the impression that he was at peace with himself and the world. He was a gifted listener; with his chin resting in his hand, he never let his gaze stray from people's faces as they spoke, his expression mirroring empathy and patience, humor and sadness. Adrienne wished that he were around for Amanda right now; he, too, had lost a spouse, and she thought Amanda would listen to him, if only because he knew how hard it really was.

A month-ago, when Adrienne had gently tried to talk to Amanda about what she was going through, Amanda had stood from the table with an angry shake of her head.

"This isn't like you and Dad," she'd said. "You two couldn't work out your problems, so you divorced. But I loved Brent. I'll always love Brent, and I lost him. You don't know what it's like to live through something like that."

Adrienne had said nothing, but when Amanda left the room, Adrienne had lowered head and whispered a single word.

Rodanthe.

While Adrienne sympathized with her daughter, she was concerned about Amanda's children. Max was six, Greg was four, and in the past eight months, Adrienne had noticed distinct changes in their personalities. Both had become un-usually withdrawn and quiet. Neither had played soccer in the fall, and though

Max was doing well in kindergarten, he cried every morning before he had to go. Greg had started to wet the bed again and would fly into tantrums at the slightest provocation. Some of these changes stemmed from the loss of their father, Adrienne knew, but they also reflected the person that Amanda had become since last spring.

Because of the insurance, Amanda didn't have to work. Nonetheless, for the first couple of months after Brent had died, Adrienne spent nearly every day at their house, keeping the bills in order and preparing meals for the children, while Amanda slept and wept in her room. She held her daughter whenever Amanda needed it, listened when Amanda wanted to talk, and forced her daughter to spend at least an hour or two outside each day, in the belief that fresh air would remind her daughter that she could begin anew.

Adrienne had thought her daughter was getting better. By early summer, Amanda had begun to smile again, infrequently at first, then a little more often. She ventured out into the town a few times, took the kids roller-skating, and Adrienne gradually began pulling back from the duties she was shouldering. It was important, she knew, for Amanda to resume responsibility for her own life again. Comfort could be found in the steady routines of life, Adrienne had learned; she hoped that by decreasing her presence in her daughter's life, Amanda would be forced to realize that, too.

But in August, on the day that would have been her seventh wedding anniversary, Amanda opened the closet door in the master bedroom, saw dust collecting on the shoulders of Brent's suits, and suddenly stopped improving. She didn't exactly regress—there were still moments when she seemed her old self—but for the most part, she seemed to be frozen somewhere in between. She was neither depressed nor happy, neither excited nor languid, neither interested nor bored by anything around her. To Adrienne, it

seemed as if Amanda had become convinced that moving forward would
somehow tarnish her memories of Brent,
and she'd made the decision not to allow
that to happen.

But it wasn't fair to the children. They
needed her guidance and her love, they
needed her attention. They needed her
to tell them that everything was going to
be all right. They'd already lost one parent, and that was hard enough. But lately,
it seemed to Adrienne that they'd lost
their mother as well.

———

In the gentle hue of the soft-lit kitchen,
Adrienne glanced at her watch. At her
request, Dan had taken Max and Greg to
the movies, so she could spend the
evening with Amanda. Like Adrienne,
both of her sons were worried about
Amanda's kids. Not only had they made
extra efforts to stay active in the boys'
lives, but nearly all of their recent con-

versations with Adrienne had begun or ended with the same question: *What do we do?*

Today, when Dan had asked the same question again, Adrienne had reassured him that she'd talk to Amanda. Though Dan had been skeptical—hadn't they tried that all along?—tonight, she knew, would be different.

Adrienne had few illusions about what her children thought of her. Yes, they loved her and respected her as a mother, but she knew they would never really *know* her. In the eyes of her children, she was kind but predictable, sweet and stable, a friendly soul from another era who'd made her way throw life with her naive view of the world intact. She looked the part, of course—veins beginning to show on the tops of her hands, a figure more like a square than an hourglass, and glasses grown thicker over the years—but when she saw them staring at her with expressions meant to humor her, she sometimes had to stifle a laugh.

Part of their error, she knew, stemmed from their desire to see her in a certain way, a preformed image they found acceptable for a woman her age. It was easier—and frankly, more comfortable—to think their mom was more sedate than daring, more of a plodder than someone with experiences that would surprise them. And in keeping with the kind, predictable, sweet, and stable mother that she was, she'd had no desire to change their minds.

Knowing that Amanda would be arriving any minute, Adrienne went to the refrigerator and set a bottle of pinot grigio on the table. The house had cooled since the afternoon, so she turned up the thermostat on her way to the bedroom.

Once the room she'd shared with Jack, it was hers now, redecorated twice since the divorce. Adrienne made her way to the four-poster bed she'd wanted ever since she was young. Wedged against the wall beneath the bed was a small stationery box, and Adrienne set it on the pillow beside her.

Inside were those things she had saved: the note he'd left at the Inn, a snapshot of him that had been taken at the clinic, and the letter she'd received a few weeks before Christmas. Beneath those items were two bundled stacks, missives written between them, that sandwiched a conch they'd once found at the beach.

Adrienne set the note off to the side and pulled an envelope from one of the stacks, remembering how she'd felt when she'd first read it, then slid out the page. It had thinned and brittled, and though the ink had faded in the years since he'd first written it, his words were still clear.

Dear Adrienne,

I've never been good at writing letters, so I hope you'll forgive me if I'm not able to make myself clear.

I arrived this morning on a donkey, believe it or not, and found out where I'd be spending my days for a while. I wish I could tell you that it was better than I imagined it would be, but in all honesty, I can't. The clinic is short of just about everything—medicine, equipment, and the necessary beds—but I spoke to the director and I think I'll be able to rectify at least part of the problem. Though they have a generator to provide electricity, there aren't any phones, so I won't be able to call until I head into Esmeraldas. It's a couple of days' ride from here, and the next supply run isn't for a few weeks. I'm sorry about that, but I think we both suspected it might be this way.

I haven't seen Mark yet. He's been at an outreach clinic in the mountains and won't be back until later this evening. I'll let you know how that goes, but I'm not expecting much at first. Like you said, I think we need to spend some time getting to know each other before we can work on the problems between us.

I can't even begin to count how many

patients I saw today. Over a hundred, I'd guess. It's been a long time since I've seen patients in this way with these types of problems, but the nurse was helpful, even when I seemed lost. I think she was thankful that I was there at all.

I've been thinking about you constantly since I left, wondering why the journey I'm on seemed to have led through you. I know my journey's not over yet, and that life is a winding path, but I can only hope it somehow circles back to the place I belong.

That's how I think of it now. I belong with you. While I was driving, and again when the plane was in the air, I imagined that when I arrived in Quito, I'd see you in the crowds waiting for me. I knew that would be impossible, but for some reason, it made leaving you just a little easier. It was almost as if part of you had come with me.

I want to believe that's true. No, change that—I know it's true. Before we met, I was as lost as a person could be, and yet you saw something in me that somehow gave me direction again. We both know the reason I went to Rodanthe, but I can't stop thinking that greater forces were at work. I went there to close a chapter in my life, hoping it would help me find my way. But it was you, I think, that I had been looking for all along. And it's you who is with me now.

We both know I have to be here for a while. I'm not sure when I'll be back, and even though it hasn't been long, I realize that I miss you more than I've ever missed anyone. Part of me yearns to jump on a plane and come to see you now, but if this is as real as I think it is, I'm sure we can make it. And I will be back, I promise you. In the short time we spent together, we had what most people can only dream about, and I'm counting the days until I can see you again. Never forget how much I love you.

Paul

When she finished reading, Adrienne set aside the letter and reached for the conch they'd stumbled across on a long-ago Sunday afternoon. Even now it smelled of brine, of timelessness, of the primordial scent of life itself. It was medium sized, perfectly formed, and without cracks, something nearly impossible to find in the rough surf of the Outer Banks after a storm. An omen, she'd thought then, and she remembered lifting it to her ear and saying that she could hear the sound of the ocean. At that, Paul had laughed, explaining that it *was* the ocean she was hearing. He'd put his arms around her then and whispered: "It's high tide, or didn't you notice?"

Adrienne thumbed through the other contents, removing what she needed for her talk with Amanda, wishing she had more time with the rest of it. Maybe later, she thought. She slid the remaining items into the bottom drawer, knowing there was no need for Amanda to see those things. Grabbing the box, Adrienne stood from the bed and smoothed her skirt.

Her daughter would be arriving shortly.

Two

———◆———

Adrienne was in the kitchen when she heard the front door open and close; a moment later, Amanda was moving through the living room.

"Mom?"

Adrienne set the box on the kitchen counter. "In here," she called.

When Amanda pushed through the swinging doors into the kitchen, she found her mother sitting at the table, an unopened bottle of wine before her.

"What's going on?" Amanda asked.

Adrienne smiled, thinking how pretty her daughter was. With light brown hair and hazel eyes to offset her high cheekbones, she had always been lovely. Though an inch shorter than Adrienne, she carried herself with the posture of a dancer and seemed taller. She was thin, too, a little too thin in Adrienne's opinion, but Adrienne had learned not to comment on it.

"I wanted to talk to you," Adrienne said.

"About what?"

Instead of answering, Adrienne motioned to the table. "I think you should sit down."

Amanda joined her at the table. Up close, Amanda looked drawn, and Adrienne reached for her hand. She squeezed it, saying nothing, then reluctantly let go as she turned toward the window. For a long moment, there were no sounds in the kitchen.

"Mom?" Amanda finally asked. "Are you okay?"

Adrienne closed her eyes and nodded. "I'm fine. I was just wondering where to begin."

Amanda stiffened slightly. "Is this about me again? Because if it is—"

Adrienne cut her off with a shake of her head. "No, this is about me," she said. "I'm going to tell you about something that happened fourteen years ago."

Amanda tilted her head, and in the familiar surroundings of the small kitchen, Adrienne began her story.

Three

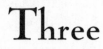

Rodanthe, 1988

The morning sky was gray when Paul Flanner left the attorney's office. Zipping his jacket, he walked through the mist to his rented Toyota Camry and slipped behind the wheel, thinking that the life he'd led for the past quarter century had formally ended with his signature on the sales contract.

It was early January 1988, and in the past month, he'd sold both his cars, his medical practice, and now, in this final meeting with his attorney, his home.

He hadn't known how he would feel about selling the house, but as he'd turned the key, he'd realized he didn't feel much of anything, other than a vague sense of completion. Earlier that morning, he'd walked through the house, room by room, one last time, hoping to remember scenes from his life. He'd thought he'd picture the Christmas tree and recall how excited his son had been when he padded downstairs in his pajamas to see the gifts that Santa had brought. He'd tried to recall the smells in the kitchen on Thanksgiving, or rainy Sunday afternoons when Martha had cooked stew, or the sounds of voices that emanated from the living room where he and his wife had hosted dozens of parties.

But as he passed from room to room, pausing a moment here and there to close his eyes, no memories sprang to life. The house, he realized, was nothing more than an empty shell, and he wondered once again why he had lived there as long as he had.

Paul exited the parking lot, turned into traffic, and made his way to the interstate, avoiding the rush of commuters coming in from the suburbs. Twenty minutes later, he turned onto Highway 70, a two-lane road that cut southeast, toward the coast of North Carolina. On the backseat, there were two large duffel bags. His airline tickets and passport were in the leather pouch on the front seat beside him. In the trunk was a medical kit and various supplies he'd been asked to bring.

Outside, the sky was a canvas of white and gray, and winter had firmly settled in. It had rained this morning for an hour, and the northerly wind made it feel colder than it was. It was neither crowded on the highway nor slick, and Paul set the cruise control a few miles over the speed limit, letting his thoughts drift back to what he had done that morning.

Britt Blackerby, his attorney, had tried one last time to talk him out of it. They'd been friends for years; six months ago, when Paul first brought up all that he

wanted to do, Britt thought Paul was kidding and laughed aloud, saying, "That'll
be the day." Only when he'd looked
across the table at the face of his friend
had he realized Paul was serious.

Paul had been prepared for that meeting, of course. It was the one habit he
couldn't shake, and he pushed three
neatly typed pages across the table, outlining what he thought were fair prices
and his specific thoughts on the proposed
contracts. Britt had stared at them for a
long moment before looking up.

"Is this because of Martha?" Britt had
asked.

"No," he'd answered, "it's just something I need to do."

In the car, Paul turned on the heater
and held his hand in front of the vent,
letting the air warm his fingers. Peeking
in the rearview mirror, he saw the sky-
scrapers of Raleigh and wondered when
he would see them again.

He'd sold the house to a young pro-
fessional couple—the husband was an

executive with GlaxoSmithKline, the wife was a psychologist—who'd seen the home on the first day it was listed. They'd come back the following day and had made an offer within hours of that visit. They were the first, and only, couple to have walked through the house.

Paul wasn't surprised. He'd been there the second time they'd walked through, and they'd spent an hour going over the features of the home. Despite their attempts to mask their feelings, Paul knew they'd buy it as soon as he'd met them. Paul showed them the features of the security system and how to open the gate that separated this neighborhood from the rest of the community; he offered the name and business card of the landscaper he used, as well as the pool maintenance company, with which he was still under contract. He explained that the marble in the foyer had been imported from Italy and that the stained-glass windows had been crafted by an artisan in Geneva. The kitchen had been remodeled only

two years earlier; the Sub Zero refrigerator and Viking cooking range were still
considered state of the art; no, he'd said,
cooking for twenty or more wouldn't be
a problem. He walked them through the
master suite and bath, then the other
bedrooms, noticing how their eyes lingered on the hand-carved molding and
sponge-painted walls. Downstairs, he
pointed out the custom furniture and
crystal chandelier and let them examine
the Persian carpet beneath the cherry
table in the formal dining room. In the
library, Paul watched as the husband ran
his fingers over the maple paneling, then
stared at the Tiffany lamp on the corner
of the desk.

"And the price," the husband said, "in-
cludes all the furniture?"

Paul nodded. As he left the library, he
could hear their hushed, excited whispers as they followed him.

Toward the end of the hour, as they
were standing at the door and getting

ready to leave, they asked the question that Paul had known was coming.

"Why are you selling?"

Paul remembered looking at the husband, knowing there was more to the question than simple curiosity. There seemed to be a hint of scandal about what Paul was doing, and the price, he knew, was far too low, even had the home been sold empty.

Paul could have said that since he was alone, he had no need for a house this big anymore. Or that the home was more suited to someone younger, who didn't mind the stairs. Or that he was planning to buy or build a different home and wanted a different decor. Or that he planned to retire, and all this was too much to take care of.

But none of those reasons were true. Instead of answering, he met the husband's eyes.

"Why do you want to buy?" he asked instead.

His tone was friendly, and the husband took a moment to glance at his wife. She was pretty, a petite brunette about the same age as her husband, mid-thirties or so. The husband was good-looking as well and stood ramrod straight, an obvious up-and-comer who had never lacked for confidence. For a moment, they didn't seem to understand what he meant.

"It's the kind of house we've always dreamed about," the wife finally answered.

Paul nodded. Yes, he thought, I remember feeling that way, too. Until six months ago, anyway.

"Then I hope it makes you happy," he said.

A moment later the couple turned to leave, and Paul watched them head to their car. He waved before closing the door, but once inside, he felt his throat constrict. Staring at the husband, he realized, had reminded him of the way he'd once felt when looking at himself in the mirror. And, for a reason he couldn't quite explain, Paul suddenly realized there were tears in his eyes.

———

The highway passed through Smithfield, Goldsboro, and Kinston, small towns separated by thirty miles of cotton and tobacco fields. He'd grown up in this part of the world, on a small farm outside Williamston, and the landmarks here were familiar to him. He rolled past tottering tobacco barns and farmhouses; he saw clusters of mistletoe in the high barren branches of oak trees just off the highway. Loblolly pines, clustered in long, thin strands, separated one property from the next.

In New Bern, a quaint town situated at the confluence of the Neuse and Trent Rivers, he stopped for lunch. From a deli in the historic district, he bought a sandwich and cup of coffee, and despite the chill, he settled on a bench near the

Sheraton that overlooked the marina. Yachts and sailboats were moored in their slips, rocking slightly in the breeze.

Paul's breaths puffed out in little clouds. After finishing his sandwich, he removed the lid from his cup of coffee. Watching the steam rise, he wondered about the turn of events that had brought him to this point.

It had been a long journey, he mused. His mother had died in childbirth, and as the only son of a father who farmed for a living, it hadn't been easy. Instead of playing baseball with friends or fishing for largemouth bass and catfish, he'd spent his days weeding and peeling boll weevils from tobacco leaves twelve hours a day, beneath a balled-up southern summer sun that permanently stained his back a golden brown. Like all children, he sometimes complained, but for the most part, he accepted the work. He knew his father needed his help, and his father was a good man. He was patient and kind, but like his own father before him, he seldom spoke unless he had reason. More often than not, their small house offered the quietude normally found in a church. Other than perfunctory questions as to how school was going or what was happening in the fields, dinners were punctuated only by the sounds of silverware tapping against the plates. After washing the dishes, his father would migrate to the living room and peruse farm reports, while Paul immersed himself in books. They didn't have a television, and the radio was seldom turned on, except for finding out about the weather.

They were poor, and though he always had enough to eat and a warm room to sleep, Paul was sometimes embarrassed by the clothes he wore or the fact that he never had enough money to head to the drugstore to buy a MoonPie or a bottle of cola like his friends. Now and then he heard snide comments about those things, but instead of fighting back, Paul devoted himself to his studies, as if trying to prove it didn't matter. Year after year, he brought home perfect grades, and though his father was proud of his accomplishments, there was an air of melancholy about him whenever he looked over Paul's report cards, as though he knew that they meant his son would one day leave the farm and never come back.

The work habits honed in the fields extended to other areas of Paul's life. Not only did he graduate valedictorian of his class, he became an excellent athlete as well. When he was cut from the football team as a freshman, the coach recommended that he try cross-country running. When he realized that effort, not genetics, usually separated the winners from losers in races, he started rising at five in the morning so he could squeeze two workouts into a day. It worked; he attended Duke University on a full athletic scholarship and was their top runner for four years, in addition to excelling in the classroom. In his four years there, he relaxed his vigilance once and nearly died as a result, but he never let it happen again. He double majored in chemistry and biology and graduated summa cum laude. That year he also became an all-American by finishing third at the national cross-country meet.

After the race, he gave the medal to his father and said that he had done all this for him.

"No," his father replied, "you ran for you. I just hope you're running toward something, not away from something."

That night, Paul stared at the ceiling as he lay in bed, trying to figure out what his father had meant. In his mind, he was running toward something, toward everything. A better life. Financial stability. A way to help his father. Respect. Freedom from worry. Happiness.

In February of his senior year, after learning he'd been accepted to medical school at Vanderbilt, he went to visit his father and told him the good news. His father said that he was pleased for him. But later that night, long after his father should have been asleep, Paul looked out the window and saw his father, a lonely figure standing near the fence post, staring out over the fields.

Three weeks later, his father died of a heart attack while tilling in preparation for the spring.

Paul was devastated by the loss, but instead of taking time to mourn, he avoided his memories by throwing himself even further into work. He enrolled at Vanderbilt early, went to summer school and took three classes to get ahead in his studies, then added extra classes in the fall to an already full schedule. After that, his life became a blur. He went to class, did his labwork, and studied until the early morning hours. He ran five miles a day and always timed his runs, trying to improve with each passing year. He avoided nightclubs and bars; he ignored the goings-on of the school athletic teams. He bought a television on a whim, but he never unpacked it from the box and sold it a year later. Though shy around girls, he was introduced to Martha, a sweet-tempered blonde from Georgia who was working at the medical school library, and when he never got around to asking her out, she took it upon herself to do so. Though worried about the frantic pace he held himself to, she nonetheless accepted his proposal, and they walked the aisle ten months later. With finals looming, there was no time for a honeymoon, but he promised they'd head someplace nice when school was out. They never got around to it. Mark, their son, was born a year later, and in the first two years of his son's life, Paul never once changed a diaper or rocked the boy to sleep.

Rather, he studied at the kitchen table, staring at diagrams of human physiology or studying chemical equations, taking notes, and acing one exam after the next. He graduated at the top of his class in three years and moved the family to Baltimore to do his surgical residency at Johns Hopkins.

Surgery, he knew by then, was his calling. Many specialties require a great deal of human interaction and hand-holding; Paul was not particularly good at either. But surgery was different; patients weren't as interested in communication skills as they were in ability, and Paul had not only the confidence to put them at ease before the operation, but the skill to do whatever was required. He thrived in that environment. In the last two years of his residency, Paul worked ninety hours a week and slept four hours a night but, oddly, showed no signs of fatigue.

After his residency, he completed a fellowship in cranial-facial surgery and moved the family to Raleigh, where he joined a practice with another surgeon just as the population was beginning to boom. As the only specialists in that field in the community, their practice grew. By thirty-four, he'd paid off his debts from medical school. By thirty-six, he was associated with every major hospital in the area and did the bulk of his work at the University of North Carolina Medical Center. There, he participated in a joint clinical study with physicians from the Mayo Clinic on neurofibromas. A year later, he had an article published in the *New England Journal of Medicine* concerning cleft palates. Another article on hemangiomas followed four months later and helped to redefine surgical procedures for infants in that field. His reputation grew, and after operating successfully on the Senator Norton's daughter, who'd been disfigured in a car accident, he made the front page of *The Wall Street Journal*.

In addition to reconstructive work, he was one of the first physicians in North Carolina to expand his practice to include plastic surgery, and he caught the wave just as it started to swell. His practice boomed, his income multiplied, and he started to accumulate things. He purchased a BMW, then a Mercedes, then a Porsche, then another Mercedes. He and Martha built the home of their dreams.

He bought stocks and bonds and shares in a dozen different mutual funds. When he realized he couldn't keep up with the intricacies of the market, he hired a money manager. After that, his money began doubling every four years. Then, when he had more than he'd ever need for the rest of his life, it began to triple.

And still he worked. He scheduled surgeries not only during the week, but on Saturday as well. He spent Sunday afternoons in the office. By the time he was forty-five, the pace he kept eventually burned out his partner, who left to work with another group of doctors.

In the first few years after Mark was born, Martha often talked about having another child. In time, she stopped bringing it up. Though she forced him to take vacations, he did so reluctantly, and in the end, she took to visiting her parents with Mark and leaving Paul at home. Paul found time to go to some of the major events in his son's life, those things that happened once or twice a year, but he missed most everything else.

He convinced himself that he was working for the family. Or for Martha, who'd struggled with him in the early years. Or for the memory of his father. Or for Mark's future. But deep down, he knew he was doing it for himself.

If he could list his major regret about those years now, it was about his son; yet despite Paul's absence from his life, Mark surprised him by deciding to become a doctor. After Mark had been accepted to medical school, Paul spread the word around the hospital corridors, pleased by the thought that his son would join him in the profession. Now, he thought, they would have more time together, and he remembered taking Mark to lunch in the hopes of convincing him to become a surgeon. Mark simply shook his head.

"That's your life," Mark had told him, "and it's not a life that interests me at all. To be honest, I feel sorry for you."

The words stung. They had an argument. Mark made bitter accusations, Paul grew furious, and Mark ended up storming out of the restaurant. Paul refused to talk to him for the next couple of weeks, and Mark made no attempt to make amends. Weeks turned into months, then into years. Though Mark continued the warm relationship he had with his mother, he avoided coming home when he knew his father was around.

Paul handled the estrangement with his son in the only way he knew. His workload stayed the same, he ran his usual five miles a day; in the mornings, he studied the financial pages in the newspaper. But he could see the sadness in Martha's eyes, and there were moments, usually late at night, when he wondered how to repair the rift with his son. Part of him wanted to pick up the phone and call, but he never found the will to do so. Mark, he knew from Martha, was doing fine without him. Instead of becoming a surgeon,

Mark became a family practitioner, and after taking several months to develop the skills he needed, he left the country to volunteer his services to an international relief organization. Though it was noble, Paul couldn't help but think he'd done it to be as far away from his father as possible.

Two weeks after he'd gone, Martha filed for divorce.

If Mark's words had once made him angry, Martha's words left him stunned. He started to try to talk her out of it, but Martha gently cut him off.

"Will you really miss me?" she said. "We hardly know each other anymore."

"I can change," he said.

Martha smiled. "I know you can. And you should. But you should do it because you want to, not because you think I want you to."

Paul spent the next couple of weeks in a daze, and a month after that, after he had completed a routine operation, sixty-two-year-old Jill Torrelson of Rodanthe, North Carolina, died in the recovery room.

It was that terrible event, following on the heels of the others, he knew, that had led him to this road now.

———◆———

After finishing his coffee, Paul got back in the car and made his way to the highway again. In forty-five minutes, he'd reached Morehead City. He crossed over the bridge to Beaufort, followed the turns, then headed down east, toward Cedar Point.

There was a peaceful beauty to the coastal lowlands, and he slowed the car, taking it all in. Life, he knew, was different here. As he drove, he marveled at the people driving in the opposite direction who waved at him, and the group of older men, sitting on a bench outside a gas station, who seemed to have nothing better to do than watch the cars pass by.

In midafternoon, he caught the ferry to Ocracoke, a village at the southern end of the Outer Banks. There were only four other cars on the ferry, and on the two-hour ride, he visited with a few of the other passengers. He spent the night at a motel in Ocracoke, woke when the white ball of light rose over the water, had an early breakfast, and then spent the next few hours walking through the rustic village, watching people ready their homes for the storm brewing off the coast.

When he was finally ready, he tossed the duffel bag into his car and began the drive northward, to the place he had to go.

The Outer Banks, he thought, were both strange and mystical. With saw grass speckling the rolling dunes and maritime oaks bent sideways with the never-ending sea breeze, it was a place like no other. The islands had once been connected to the mainland, but after the last ice age, the sea had flooded the area to

the immediate west, forming the Pamlico Sound. Until the 1950s, there wasn't
a highway on this series of islands, and
people had to drive along the beach to
reach the homes beyond the dunes. Even
now it was part of the culture, and as he
drove, he could see tire tracks near the
water's edge.

The sky had cleared in places, and though
the clouds raced angrily toward the horizon, the sun sometimes squinted through,
making the world glow fiercely white.
Over the roar of the engine, he could hear
the violence of the ocean.

At this time of year, the Outer Banks
were largely empty, and he had this
stretch of roadway to himself. In the soli-
tude, his thoughts returned to Martha.

The divorce had become final only a
few months earlier, but it had been ami-
cable. He knew she was seeing someone,
and he suspected she'd been seeing him
even before they'd separated, but it
wasn't important. These days, nothing
seemed important.

When she left, Paul remembered cutting back on his schedule, thinking he needed time to sort things out. But months later, instead of going back to his regular routine, he cut back even more. He still ran regularly but found he no longer had any interest in reading the financial pages in the morning. For as long as he could remember, he'd needed only six hours of sleep a night; but strangely, the more he cut back on the pace of his previous life, the more hours he seemed to need to feel rested.

There were other, physical changes as well. For the first time in years, Paul felt the muscles in his shoulders relax. The lines in his face, grown deep over the years, were still prominent, but the intensity he once saw in his reflection had been replaced with a sort of weary melancholy. And though it was probably his imagination, it seemed as if his graying hair had finally stopped receding.

At one time, he had thought he had it all. He'd run and run, he'd reached the pinnacle of success; yet now, he realized he'd never taken his father's advice. All his life, he'd been running away from something, not toward something, and in his heart, he knew it had all been in vain.

He was fifty-four and alone in the world, and as he stared at the vacant stretch of asphalt unfolding before him, he couldn't help but wonder why on earth he'd run so hard.

———◆———

Knowing he was close now, Paul settled in for the final leg of his journey. He was staying at a small bed-and-breakfast just off the highway, and when he reached the outskirts of Rodanthe, he took in his surroundings. Downtown, if you could call it that, consisted of various businesses that seemed to offer just about everything. The general store sold hardware and fishing gear as well as groceries; the gas station sold tires and auto parts as well as the services of a mechanic.

He had no reason to ask for directions, and a minute later, he pulled off the highway onto a short, gravel drive, thinking the Inn at Rodanthe was more charming than he'd imagined it would be. It was an aging white Victorian with black shutters and a welcoming front porch. On the railings were potted pansies in full bloom, and an American flag fluttered in the wind.

He grabbed his gear and slung the bags over his shoulder, then walked up the steps and went inside. The floor was heart pine, scuffed by years of sandy feet, and without the formality of his former home. On his left, there was a cozy sitting room, brightly lit by two large windows framing the fireplace. He could smell fresh coffee and saw that a small platter of cookies had been set out for his arrival. On the right, he assumed he'd find the proprietor, and he went that way.

Though he saw a small desk where he was supposed to check in, no one was behind it. In the corner behind it, he saw the room keys; the key chains were small statues of lighthouses. When he reached the desk, he rang the bell, requesting service.

He waited, then rang again, and this time he heard what sounded like a muffled cry coming from somewhere in the rear of the house. Leaving his gear, he stepped around the desk and pushed through a set of swinging doors that led to the kitchen. On the counter were three unpacked grocery bags.

The backdoor was open, beckoning him that way, and the porch creaked as he stepped outside. On the left, he saw a couple of rocking chairs and a small table between them; on the right, he saw the source of the noise.

She was standing in the corner; overlooking the ocean. Like him, she was wearing faded jeans, but she was enveloped by a thick turtleneck sweater. Her light brown hair was pinned back, a few loose tendrils whipping in the wind. He watched as she turned, startled at the sound of his boots on the porch. Behind her, a dozen terns rode the updrafts, and a coffee cup was perched on the railing.

Paul glanced away, then found his eyes drawn to her again. Even though she was crying, he could tell she was pretty, but there was something in the sad way she shifted her weight that let him know she didn't realize it. And that, he would always think when looking back on this moment, had only served to make her even more appealing.

Four

———◆———

Amanda looked across the table at her mother.

Adrienne had paused and was staring out the window again. The rain had stopped; beyond the glass, the sky was full of shadows. In the silence, Amanda could hear the refrigerator humming steadily.

"Why are you telling me this, Mom?"

"Because I think you need to hear it."

"But why? I mean, who was he?"

Instead of answering, Adrienne reached for the bottle of wine. With deliberate motions, she opened it. After pouring herself a glass, she did the same for her daughter.

"You might need this," she said.

"Mom?"

Adrienne slid the glass across the table.

"Do you remember when I went to Rodanthe? When Jean asked if I could watch the Inn?"

It took a moment before it clicked.

"Back when I was in high school, you mean?"

"Yes."

When Adrienne began again, Amanda found herself reaching for her wine, wondering what this was all about.

Five

———⊰•⊱———

Standing near the railing on the back
porch of the Inn on a gloomy Thursday
afternoon, Adrienne let the coffee cup
warm her hands as she stared at the
ocean, noting that it was rougher than it
had been an hour earlier. The water had
taken on the color of iron, like the hull
of old battleships, and she could see tiny
whitecaps stretching to the horizon.

Part of her wished she hadn't come.
She was watching the Inn for a friend,
and she'd hoped it would be a respite of
sorts, but now it seemed like a mistake.
First, the weather wasn't going to
cooperate—all day, the radio had been

warning of the big nor'easter heading this way—and she wasn't looking forward to the possibility of losing power or having to hole up inside for a couple of days. But more than that, despite the angry skies, the beach brought back memories of too many family vacations, blissful days when she'd been content with the world.

For a long time, she'd considered herself lucky. She'd met Jack as a student; he was in his first year of law school. They were considered a perfect couple back then—he was tall and thin, with curly black hair; she was a blue-eyed brunette a few sizes smaller than she was now. Their wedding photo had been prominently displayed in the living room of their home, right above the fireplace. They had their first child when she was twenty-eight and had two more in the next three years. She, like so many other women, had trouble losing all the weight she'd gained, but she worked at it, and though she never approached what she had once been, compared to most of the women her age with children, she thought she was doing okay.

And she was happy. She loved to cook, she kept the house clean, they went to church as a family, and she did her best to maintain an active social life for her and Jack. When the kids started going to school, she volunteered to help in their classes, attended PTA meetings, worked in their Sunday school, and was the first to volunteer when rides were needed for field trips. She sat through hours of piano recitals, school plays, baseball and football games, she taught each of the children to swim, and she laughed aloud at the expression on their faces the first time they walked through the gates of Disney World. On her fortieth birthday, Jack had thrown a surprise party for her at the country club, and nearly two hundred people showed up. It was an evening filled with laughter and high spirits, but later, after they got home, she noticed that Jack didn't watch her as she undressed before getting into bed. Instead, he turned out the lights, and though she knew he couldn't fall asleep that quickly, he pretended he had.

Looking back, she knew it should have tipped her off that all was not as it seemed, but with three children and a husband who left the child rearing up to her, she was too busy to ponder it. Besides, she neither expected nor believed that the passion between them would never go through down periods. She'd been married long enough to know better. She assumed it would return as it always had, and she wasn't worried about it. But it didn't. By forty-one, she'd become concerned about their relationship and had started perusing the self-help section of the bookstore, looking for titles that might advise her on how to improve their marriage, and she sometimes found herself looking toward the future when things might slow down. She imagined what it would be like to be a grandmother or what she and Jack might do when they had the time to enjoy each other's company as a couple again. Maybe then, she thought, things would go back to what they had once been.

It was around that time that she saw Jack having lunch with Linda Gaston. Linda, she knew, worked with Jack's firm at their branch office in Greensboro. Though she specialized in estate law while Jack worked in general litigation, Adrienne knew their cases sometimes overlapped and required a collaboration, so it didn't surprise her to see them dining with each other. Adrienne even smiled at them through the window. Though Linda wasn't a close friend, she'd been a guest in their home numerous times, and they'd always gotten along well, despite the fact that Linda was ten years younger and single. It was only when she went inside the restaurant that she noticed the tender way they were looking at each other. And she knew with certainty they were holding hands under the table.

For a long moment, Adrienne stood frozen in place, but instead of confronting them, she turned around and headed out before they had a chance to see her.

In denial, she cooked Jack's favorite meal that night and mentioned nothing about what she'd seen. She pretended it hadn't happened, and in time, she was able to convince herself that she'd been mistaken about what was going on between them. Maybe Linda was going through a hard time and he was comforting her. Jack was like that. Or maybe, she thought, it was a fleeting fantasy that neither of them had acted on, a romance of the mind and nothing else.

But it wasn't. Their marriage began spiraling downward, and within a few months, Jack asked for a divorce. He was in love with Linda, he said. He hadn't meant for it to happen, and he hoped she would understand. She didn't and said so, but when she was forty-two, Jack moved out.

Now, over three years later, Jack had moved on, but Adrienne found it impossible to do. Though they had joint custody, it was joint in name only. Jack lived in Greensboro, and the three-hour drive was just long enough to keep the kids with her most of the time. Mostly he was thankful for that, but the pressures of raising them on her own tested her limits daily. At night, she often collapsed in bed but found it impossible to sleep because she couldn't stop the questions that rolled through her mind. And though she never told anyone, she sometimes imagined what she would say if Jack showed up at the door and asked her to take him back, knowing that deep down, she would probably say yes.

She hated herself for that, but what could she do?

She didn't want this life; she'd neither asked for it nor expected it. Nor, she thought, did she deserve it. She'd played by the book, she'd followed the rules. For eighteen years, she'd been faithful.

She'd overlooked those times when he drank too much, she brought him coffee when he had to work late, and she never said a word when he went golfing on the weekends instead of spending time with the kids.

Was it just the sex he was after? Sure, Linda was both younger and prettier, but was it really that important to him that he'd throw away everything else in his life? Didn't the kids mean anything? Didn't she? Didn't the eighteen years together? And anyway, it wasn't as if she'd lost interest—in the last couple of years whenever they'd made love, she'd been the one to initiate it. If the urge was so strong, why hadn't he done something about it?

Or was it, she wondered, that he found her boring? Granted, because they'd been married so long, there weren't a lot of new stories to tell. Over the years, most had been recycled in slightly different versions, and both had reached the point where they knew the endings in advance, after only a few words. Instead, they did what she thought most couples did: She'd ask how work had gone, he'd ask about the kids, and they'd talk about the latest antics of one family member or another or what was happening around town. There were times that even she wished there were something more interesting to talk about, but didn't he understand that in a few years the same thing was going to happen with Linda?

It wasn't fair. Even her friends had said as much, and she assumed that meant they were on her side. And maybe they were, but they had a funny way of showing it, she thought. A month ago, she'd gone to a Christmas party hosted by a couple she'd known for years, and who should happen to be there but Jack and Linda. It was life in a small southern town—people forgave things like that— but Adrienne couldn't help but feel betrayed.

Beyond the hurt and betrayal, she was lonely. She hadn't been on a date since the day Jack had moved out. Rocky Mount wasn't exactly a hotbed of unmarried men in their forties, and those who were single weren't necessarily the kind of man she wanted anyway. Most of them had baggage, and she didn't think she could tote around any more than she was already carrying. In the beginning, she told herself to be selective, and when she thought she was ready to enter the world of dating again, she mentally outlined a set of traits she was looking for. She wanted someone intelligent and kind and attractive, but more than that, she wanted someone who accepted the fact that she was raising three teenagers. It might be a problem, she suspected, but since her kids were pretty self-sufficient, she didn't think it was the type of hurdle that would discourage most men.

Boy, was she ever wrong.

In the last three years, she hadn't been asked out at all, and lately she'd come to believe that she never would. Good old jack could have his fun, good old Jack could read the morning paper with someone new, but for her, it just wasn't in the cards.

And then, of course, there were the financial worries.

Jack had given her the house and paid the court-ordered support on time, but it was just enough to make ends meet. Despite the fact that Jack earned a good living while they were married, they hadn't saved as they should have. Like so many couples, they'd spent years caught up in the endless cycle of spending most of what they'd earned. They had new cars and took nice vacations; when big-screen televisions first hit the market, they were the first family in the neighborhood to have one in their home. She'd always believed that Jack was taking care of the future since he was the one who handled the bills. It turned out that he wasn't, and she'd had to take a part-time job at the local library. Though she wasn't so worried about her or the children, she was scared for her father.

A year after the divorce, her father had had a stroke, then three more in rapid succession. Now he needed around-the-clock care. The nursing home she'd found for him was excellent, but as an only child, she bore the responsibility of paying for it. She had enough left over from the settlement to cover another year, but after that, she didn't know what she would do. She was already spending everything she earned at the part-time job she'd taken at the library. When Jean had first asked if Adrienne would mind watching the Inn while she was out of town, she had suspected that Adrienne was struggling financially and had left far more money than was necessary for the groceries. The note she'd left had told Adrienne to keep the remainder as payment for her help. Adrienne appreciated that, but charity from friends hurt her pride.

Money, though, was only part of her worries about her father. She sometimes felt he was the only person who was always on her side, and she needed her father, especially now. Spending time with him was an escape of sorts for her, and she dreaded the thought that their hours together might end because of something she did or didn't do.

What would become of him? What would become of her?

Adrienne shook her head, forcing those questions away. She didn't want to think about any of this, especially row. Jean had said it would be slow—only one reservation was in the books—and she'd hoped that coming here would clear her mind. She wanted to walk the beach or read a couple of novels that had been sitting on her bedstand for months; she wanted to put her feet up and watch the porpoises playing in the waves. She had hoped to find relief, but as she stood on the porch at the sea-worn Inn at Rodanthe awaiting the oncoming storm, she felt the world bearing down hard. She was middle-aged and alone, overworked and soft around the middle. Her kids were struggling, her father was sick, and she wasn't sure how she'd be able to keep going.

That was when she started to cry, and minutes later, when she heard footsteps on the porch, she turned her head and saw Paul Flanner for the first time.

———✦———

Paul had seen people cry before, thousands of times, he would guess, but it had usually been within the sterile confines of a hospital waiting room, when he was fresh from an operation and still wearing scrubs. For him, the scrubs had served as a type of shield against the personal and emotional nature of his work. Never once had he cried with those he'd spoken with, nor could he remember any of the faces of those who had once looked to him for answers. It wasn't something that he was proud to admit, but it was the person he had once been.

But at this moment, as he looked into

the red-rimmed eyes of the woman on the porch, he felt like an intruder on unfamiliar ground. His first instinct was to throw up the old defenses. Yet there was something about the way she looked that made doing so impossible. It might have been the setting or the fact that she was alone; either way, the surge of empathy was a foreign sensation that caught him off guard.

Not having expected him to arrive until later, Adrienne tried to overcome her embarrassment at being caught in such a state. Forcing a smile, she dabbed at her tears, trying to pretend the wind had caused them to moisten.

As she turned to face him, however, she couldn't help but stare.

It was his eyes, she thought, that did it. They were light blue, so light they seemed almost translucent, but there was an intensity in them that she'd never seen before in anyone else.

He knows me, she suddenly thought. *Or could know me if I gave him a chance.*

As quickly as those thoughts came, she dismissed them, thinking them ridiculous. No, she decided, there was nothing unusual about the man standing before her. He was simply the guest Jean had told her about, and since she hadn't been at the desk, he'd come looking for her; that was all. As a result, she found herself evaluating him in the way strangers often do.

Though he wasn't as tall as Jack had been, maybe five ten or so, he was lean and fit, like someone who exercised daily. The sweater he was wearing was expensive and didn't match his faded jeans, but somehow he made it look as if it did. His face was angular, marked by lines in his forehead that spoke of years of forced concentration. His gray hair was trimmed short, and there were patches of white near his ears: she guessed he was in his fifties, but couldn't pin it down any more than that.

Just then, Paul seemed to realize he was staring at her and dropped his gaze. "I'm sorry," he murmured, "I didn't mean to interrupt." He motioned over his shoulder. "I'll wait for you inside. Take your time."

Adrienne shook her head, trying to put him at ease. "It's okay. I was planning on coming in anyway."

When she looked at him, she caught his eyes a second time. They were softer now, laced with a hint of memory, as though he were thinking of something sad but trying to hide it. She reached for her coffee cup, using it as an excuse to turn away.

When Paul held open the door, she nodded for him to go ahead. As he walked ahead of her through the kitchen toward the reception area, Adrienne caught herself eyeing his athletic physique, and she flushed slightly, wondering what on earth had gotten into her. Chiding herself, she moved behind the desk. She checked the name in the reservation book and glanced up.

"Paul Flanner, right? You're staying

five nights, and checking out Tuesday morning?"

"Yes." He hesitated. "Is it possible to get a room with a view of the ocean?"

Adrienne pulled out the registration form. "Sure. Actually, you could have any of the rooms upstairs. You're the only guest scheduled this weekend."

"Which would you recommend?"

"They're all nice, but if I were you, I'd take the blue room."

"The blue room?"

"It's got the darkest curtains. If you sleep in the yellow or white rooms, you'll be up at the crack of dawn. The shutters don't help all that much, and the sun comes up pretty early. The windows in those rooms face east." Adrienne slid the form toward him and set the pen beside it. "Could you sign here?"

"Sure."

Adrienne watched as Paul scrawled his name, thinking as he signed that his hands matched his face. The bones of his knuckles were prominent, like those of an older man, but his movements were precise and measured. He wasn't wearing a wedding ring, she saw—not that it mattered.

Paul set aside the pen and she reached for the form, making sure he'd filled it out correctly. His address was listed in care of an attorney in Raleigh. From the pegboard off to the side, she retrieved a room key, hesitated, then selected two more.

"Okay, we're all set here," she said. "You ready to see your room?"

"Please."

Paul stepped back as she made her way around the desk, toward the stairs. He grabbed his duffel bags, then started after her. When she reached the steps, she paused, letting him catch up. She motioned toward the sitting room.

"I have coffee and some cookies right over there. I made the pot an hour ago, so it should still be fresh for a while."

"I saw it when I came in. Thank you."

At the top of the steps, Adrienne

turned, her hand still resting on the balustrade. There were four rooms upstairs: one near the front of the house and three that faced the ocean. On the doors Paul saw nameplates, not numbers: Bodie, Hatteras, and Cape Lookout, and he recognized them as the names of lighthouses along the Outer Banks.

"You can take your pick," Adrienne said. "I brought all three keys in case you like another one better."

Paul looked from one room to the next. "Which one's the blue room?"

"Oh, that's just what I call it: Jean calls it the Bodie Suite."

"Jean?"

"She's the owner. I'm just watching the place while she's gone."

The straps of the duffel bags were pinching his neck, and Paul shifted them as Adrienne unlocked the door. She held the door open for him, feeling the duffel bag bump against her as he wedged by.

Paul glanced around. The room was

just about what he'd imagined it would be: simple and clean, but with more character than a typical beachfront motel room. There was a four-poster bed centered beneath the window, with an end table beside it. On the ceiling, a fan was whirring slowly, just enough to move the air. In the far corner, near a large painting of the Bodie lighthouse, there was a doorway that Paul assumed led to the bathroom. Along the near wall stood a worn-looking chest of drawers that looked as if it had been in the room since the Inn had been built.

With the exception of the furniture, pretty much everything was tinted various shades of blue: the throw rug on the floor was the color of robin's eggs, the comforter and curtains were navy, the lamp on the end table was somewhere in between and shiny, like the paint on a new car. Though the chest of drawers and the end table were eggshell, they'd been decorated with scenes of the ocean beneath summer skies. Even the phone was blue, which gave it the appearance of a toy.

"What do you think?"

"It's definitely blue," he said.

"Do you want to see the other rooms?"

Paul set the duffel bags on the floor as he looked out the window.

"No, this will be fine. Is it okay if I open the window, though? It's kind of stuffy in here."

"Go ahead."

Paul crossed the room, flipped the latch, and lifted the pane. Because the home had been painted so many times over the years, the window caught after about an inch. As Paul struggled to raise it further, Adrienne could see the wiry muscles of his forearms knot and flex.

She cleared her throat.

"I guess you should know it's my first time watching the Inn," she said. "I've been here lots of times, but always when

Jean was here, so if something's not right, don't think twice about telling me."

Paul turned around. With his back to the glass, his features were lost in shadows.

"I'm not worried," he said. "I'm not too picky these days."

Adrienne smiled as she pulled the key from the door. "Okay, things you should know. Jean told me to go over these. There's a wall heater beneath the window, and all you have to do is turn it on. There's only two settings, and in the beginning it'll make a clicking noise, but it'll stop after a few minutes. There are fresh towels in the bathroom; if you need more, just let me know. And even though it seems to take forever, the hot water does eventually come out of the nozzle. I promise."

Adrienne caught a glimpse of Paul's smile as she went on.

"And unless we get someone else this weekend—and I'm not expecting anyone else with the storm unless they get stranded," she said, "we can eat whenever you'd like. Normally, Jean serves breakfast at eight and dinner is at seven, but if you're busy then, just let me know and we can eat whenever. Or I can make you something that you could take with you."

"Thanks."

She paused, her mind searching for anything else to say.

"Oh yeah, one more thing. Before you use the phone, you should know it's only set up to make local calls. If you want to dial long distance, you'll have to use a calling card or call collect, and you'll have to go through the operator."

"Okay."

She hesitated in the doorway. "Anything else you need to know?"

"I think that just about covers it. Except, of course, for the obvious."

"What's that?"

"You haven't told me your name yet."

She set the key on the chest of drawers

beside the door and smiled. "I'm Adrienne. Adrienne Willis."

Paul crossed the room, and surprising her, he offered his hand.

"Nice to meet you, Adrienne."

Six

———⊰⊱———

Paul had come to Rodanthe at the request of Robert Torrelson, and as he unpacked a few items from the duffel bag and placed them in the drawers, he wondered again what Robert wanted to say to him or if he expected Paul to do most of the talking.

Jill Torrelson had come to him because she had a meningioma. A benign cyst, it wasn't a life-threatening ailment, but it was unsightly, to say the least. The meningioma was on the right side of her face, extending from the bridge of her nose and over the cheek, forming a bulbous purple mass, punctuated by scars where it had ulcerated over the years. Paul had operated on dozens of patients with meningiomas, and he'd received many letters from those who had undergone the operation, expressing how thankful they were for what he'd done.

He'd gone over it a thousand times, and he still didn't know why she'd died. Nor, it seemed, could science provide the answer. The autopsy on Jill was inconclusive, and the cause of death had not been determined. At first, they assumed she'd had an embolism of some sort, but they could find no evidence of it. After that, they focused on the idea that she'd had an allergic reaction to the anesthesia or postsurgical medication, but those were eventually ruled out as well. So was negligence on Paul's part; the surgery had gone off without a hitch, and a close examination by the coroner had found nothing out of the ordinary with the procedure or anything that might have been even tangentially responsible for her death.

The videotape had confirmed it. Because the meningioma was considered typical, the procedure had been video-taped by the hospital for potential use in instruction by the faculty. Afterward, it had been reviewed by the surgical board of the hospital and three additional surgeons from out of state. Again, nothing was found to be amiss.

There were some medical conditions mentioned in the report. Jill Torrelson was overweight and her arteries had thickened; in time, she may have needed a coronary bypass. She had diabetes and, as a lifelong smoker, the beginnings of emphysema, though again, neither of these conditions seemed life-threatening at present, and neither adequately explained what had happened.

Jill Torrelson, it seemed, had died for no reason at all, as if God had simply called her home.

Like so many others in his situation, Robert Torrelson had filed a wrongful death suit. The lawsuit named Paul, the

hospital, and the anesthesiologist as de-
fendants. Paul, like most surgeons, was
covered by malpractice insurance. As was
customary, he was instructed not to
speak to Robert Torrelson without an
attorney present and even then only if he
was being deposed and Robert Torrelson
happened to be in the room.

The case had gone nowhere for a year.
Once Robert Torrelson's attorney received the autopsy report, had another
surgeon review the videotape, and the
attorneys from the insurance company
and hospital started the process of filing
motions to drag out the process and run
up the costs, he'd painted a bleak picture
of what his client was up against.
Though they didn't say so directly, the
attorneys for the insurance company expected Robert Torrelson to eventually
drop the suit.

It was like the few other cases that had
been filed against Paul Flanner over the
years, except for the fact that Paul had

received a personal note from Robert Torrelson two months ago.

He didn't need to bring it with him to recall what had been written.

Dear Dr. Flanner,
   I would like to talk to you in person. This is very important to me.
                        Please.
                        Robert Torrelson

At the bottom of the letter, he'd left his address.

After reading it, Paul had showed it to the attorneys, and they'd urged him to ignore it. So had his former colleagues at the hospital. Just let it go, they'd said. Once this is over, we can set up a meeting with him if he still wants to talk.

But there was something in the simple plea above Robert Torrelson's neatly scrawled signature that had gotten to Paul, and he'd decided not to listen to them.

To his mind, he'd ignored too many things already.

———◆———

Paul put on his jacket, walked down the steps, and went out the front door, heading toward the car. From the front seat, he grabbed the leather pouch containing his passport and tickets, but instead of going back inside, he made his way around the side of the house.

On the beach side the wind grew cold, and Paul paused for a moment to zip his jacket. Pinching the leather pouch beneath his arm, he tucked his hands into his jacket and bowed his head, feeling the breeze nip at his cheeks.

The sky reminded him of those he'd seen in Baltimore before snowstorms that tinted the world into shades of washed-out gray. In the distance, he could see a pelican gliding low over the water, its wings unmoving, floating with the wind. He wondered where it would go when the storm hit full force.

Near the water, Paul stopped. The waves were rolling in from two different directions, sending up plumes as they collided. The air was moist and chilly. Glancing over his shoulder, he saw the light in the kitchen of the Inn glowing yellow. Adrienne's figure passed shadow-like by the window, then vanished from sight.

He would try to talk to Robert Torrelson tomorrow morning, he thought. The storm was expected to arrive in the afternoon and would probably last through most of the weekend, so he couldn't do it then. Nor did he want to wait until Monday; his flight left on Tuesday afternoon out of Dulles, and he had to leave Rodanthe no later than nine. He didn't want to run the risk of not speaking with him, and in light of the storm, one day was cutting it close. By Monday, power lines might be down,

there might be flooding, or Robert
Torrelson might be taking care of who
knew what in the aftermath.

Paul had never been in Rodanthe before, but he didn't think it would take
more than a few minutes to find the
house. The town, he figured, had no
more than a few dozen streets, and he
could walk the length of the town in less
than half an hour.

After a few minutes on the sand, Paul
turned and started making his way back
toward the Inn. As he did, he caught a
glimpse of Adrienne Willis in the window again.

Her smile, he thought. He liked her
smile.

———•◦•———

From the window, Adrienne found
herself glancing at Paul Flanner as he
made his way back from the beach.

She was unpacking the groceries, doing her best to put them in the right cup-

boards. Earlier in the afternoon, she'd bought the items that Jean had recommended, but now she wondered if she should have waited until Paul arrived to ask him if there was anything in particular that he wanted to eat.

His visit intrigued her. She knew from Jean that when he'd called six weeks ago, she'd said that she closed up after the New Year and wouldn't open again until April; but he'd offered to pay double the room rate if she could stay open an extra week.

He wasn't on vacation, she was sure of that. Not only because Rodanthe wasn't a popular destination in winter, but because he didn't strike her as the vacationing type. Nor was his demeanor when he'd checked in that of someone who'd come here to relax.

He hadn't mentioned that he was visiting family, either, so that meant he was probably here for business. But that, too, didn't make much sense. Other than fishing and tourism, there wasn't much business in Rodanthe, and with the exception of those businesses that provided the necessities for those who lived here, most of them closed down for the winter anyway.

She was still trying to figure it out when she heard him coming up the back steps. She listened as he stomped the sand from his feet outside the door.

A moment later, the back door opened with a squeak, and Paul walked into the kitchen. As he shrugged off his jacket, she noticed that the tip of his nose had turned red.

"I think the storm's getting close," he said. "The temperature's dropped at least ten degrees since this morning."

Adrienne put a box of croutons into the cupboard and looked over her shoulder as she answered.

"I know. I had to turn the heater up. This isn't the most energy efficient of homes. I could actually feel the wind coming in through the windows. Sorry you don't have better weather."

Paul rubbed his arms. "That's the way it goes. Is the coffee still out? I think I could use a cup to warm up."

"It might be a little stale by now. I'll make a fresh pot. It'll only take a few minutes."

"You wouldn't mind?"

"Not at all. I think I could use one, too."

"Thank you. Just let me put my jacket in my room and clean up, and I'll be right back down."

He smiled at her before he left the kitchen, and Adrienne felt herself exhale, unaware she'd been holding her breath. In his absence, she ground a handful of fresh beans, changed the filter, and started the coffee. She retrieved the silver pot, poured the contents down the sink, and rinsed it out. As she worked, she could hear him moving in the room above her.

Though she'd known in advance that he would be the only guest this week-end, she hadn't realized how strange it would seem to be alone in the house with him. Or alone, period. Sure, the kids had their own activities and she had a little time to herself now and then, but it was never for long. They could pop back in at any moment. Besides, they were *family*. It wasn't quite the same as the situation she was in now, and she couldn't escape the feeling that she was living someone else's life, one in which she wasn't exactly sure of the rules.

She made a cup of coffee for herself and poured the rest into the silver pot. She was putting the pot back on the tray in the sitting room when she heard him coming down the stairs.

"Just in time," she said. "Coffee's ready. Would you like me to get the fire going?"

As Paul entered the sitting room, she caught a trace of cologne. He reached around her for a cup.

"No, that's okay. I'm comfortable. Maybe later."

She nodded and took a small step backward. "Well, if you need anything, I'll be in the kitchen."

"I thought you said you wanted a cup."

"I already poured one. I left it on the counter."

He looked up. "You're not going to join me?"

There was something expectant in the way he asked, as if he really wanted her to stay.

She hesitated. Jean was good at making small talk with strangers, but she never had been. At the same time, she was flattered by his offer, though she wasn't sure why.

"I suppose I could," she finally said, "just let me get my cup."

By the time she'd returned, Paul was sitting in one of the two glider rockers near the fireplace. With black-and-white photographs along the wall that depicted life in the Outer Banks during the 1920s and a long shelf of thumbed-through books, this had always been her favorite room in the house. There were two windows along the far wall that looked to the ocean. A small stack of cordwood was piled near the fireplace along with a container of kindling, as if promising a cozy evening with family.

Paul was holding his cup of coffee in his lap, rocking back and forth, taking in the view. The wind was making the sand blow, and the fog was rolling in, giving the world outside an illusion of dusk. Adrienne sat in the chair next to his and for a moment watched the scene in silence, trying not to feel nervous.

Paul turned toward her. "Do you think the storm's going to blow us away tomorrow?" he asked.

Adrienne ran her hand through her hair. "I doubt it. This place has been here for sixty years, and it hasn't blown away yet."

"Have you ever been here during a nor'easter? A big one, I mean, like the one they're expecting?"

"No. But Jean has, so it can't be too

bad. But then again, she's from here, so maybe she's used to it."

As she answered, Paul found himself evaluating her. Younger by a few years than he was, with light brown hair cut just above the shoulder blades and curled slightly. She wasn't thin, but she wasn't heavy, either; to him, her figure was inviting in a way that defied the unrealistic standards of television or magazines. She had a slight bump on her nose, crows-feet around her eyes, and her skin had reached that soft point in between youth and age, before gravity began to take its toll.

"And you said she's a friend?"

"We met in college years ago. Jean was one of my roommates, and we've kept in touch ever since. This used to be her grandparents' house, but her parents converted it to an inn. After you made arrangements with her to stay, she called me, since she had an out-of-town wedding to attend."

"But you don't live here?"

"No, I live in Rocky Mount. Have you ever been there?"

"Many times. I used to pass through on trips to Greenville."

At his answer, Adrienne wondered again about the address he'd listed on the registration form. She took a sip of coffee and lowered the cup to her lap.

"I know it's none of my business," she said, "but can I ask what you're doing here? You don't have to answer if you don't want—I'm just curious."

Paul shifted in his chair. "I'm here to talk to someone."

"That's a long way to drive to have a conversation."

"I didn't have much of a choice. He wanted to meet in person."

His voice sounded tight and remote, and for a moment, he seemed lost in thought. In the silence, Adrienne could hear the whipping of the flag out front.

Paul set his coffee on the table between them.

"What do you do?" he finally asked, his voice warming again. "Besides watching bed-and-breakfasts for friends?"

"I work in the public library."

"You do?"

"You sound surprised."

"I guess I am. I expected you to say something different."

"Like what?"

"To be honest, I'm not sure. Just not that. You don't look old enough to be a librarian. Where I live, they're all in their sixties."

She smiled. "It's only part-time. I have three kids, so I do the mom thing, too."

"How old are they?"

"Eighteen, seventeen, and fifteen."

"Do they keep you busy?"

"No, not really. As long as I'm up by five and don't go to bed until it's midnight, it's not too bad."

He chuckled under his breath, and Adrienne felt herself beginning to relax. "How about you? Do you have children?"

"Just one. A son." For a moment his eyes dropped, but he came back to her again. "He's a doctor in Ecuador."

"He lives there?"

"For the time being. He's volunteering his services for a couple of years at a clinic near Esmeraldas."

"You must be proud of him."

"I am." He paused. "But to be honest, he must have gotten that from my wife. Or rather, my ex-wife. It was more her doing than mine."

Adrienne smiled. "That's nice to hear."

"What?"

"That you still appreciate her good qualities. Even though you're divorced, I mean. I don't hear a lot of people saying those things after they split up. Usually, when people talk about their exes, all they bring up are the things that went wrong or the bad things the other person did."

Paul wondered if she was speaking from personal experience, guessing that she was.

"Tell me about your kids, Adrienne. What do they like to do?"

Adrienne took another sip of her coffee, thinking how odd it was to hear him saying her name.

"My kids? Oh, well, let's see . . . Matt was the starting quarterback on the football team, and now he's playing guard on the basketball team. Amanda loves drama, and she just won the lead to play Maria in *West Side Story.* And Dan . . . well, right now, Dan is playing basketball, too, but next year, he thinks he might go out for wrestling instead. The coach has been begging him to try out since he saw him at sports camp last summer."

Paul raised his eyebrows. "Impressive."

"What can I say? It was all their mother's doing," she quipped.

"Why does that not surprise me?"

She smiled. "Of course, that's just the good part. Had I told you about their mood swings or their attitudes, or let you see their messy rooms, you'd probably think I was doing a terrible job raising them."

Paul smiled. "I doubt it. What I'd think is that you were raising teenagers."

"In other words, you're telling me that your son, the conscientious doctor, went through all this, too, so I shouldn't lose hope?"

"I'm sure he did."

"You don't know for sure, though?"

"Not really. I wasn't around as much as I should have been. There was a time in my life when I used to work too much."

She could tell it was a difficult admission for him, and she wondered why he'd said it. Before she could dwell on it, the phone rang and they both turned at the sound.

"Excuse me," she said, rising from her seat. "I have to get that."

Paul watched her walk away, noticing again how attractive she was. In spite of the direction his medical practice had taken in later years, he'd always remained less interested in appearance than those things a person couldn't see: kindness and integrity, humor and sensibility. Adrienne, he was sure, had all those traits, but he got the feeling that they'd been unappreciated for a long time, maybe even by her.

He could tell that she had been nervous when she first sat down, and he found that oddly endearing. Too often, especially in his line of work, people seemed intent on trying to impress, making sure they said the right things, showcasing those things they did well. Others rambled on, as if they viewed conversation as a one-way street, and nothing was more boring than a blowhard. None of those traits seemed to apply to Adrienne.

And, he had to admit, it was nice to talk to someone who didn't know him. During the past few months, he'd alternated between spending time alone or fending off questions as to whether or not he was feeling okay. More than once, colleagues had recommended the name of a good therapist and confided that the person had helped them. Paul had grown tired of explaining that he knew what he was doing and that he was sure of his decision. And he was even more tired of the looks of concern they offered in response.

But there was something about Adrienne that made him feel she would understand what he was going through. He couldn't explain why he felt that way or why it mattered. But either way, he was sure of it.

Seven

A few minutes later, Paul put his empty cup on the tray, then carried the tray to the kitchen.

Adrienne was still on the phone when he got there, her back toward him. She was leaning against the counter, one leg crossed over the other, twirling a strand of hair between her fingers. From her tone, he could tell she was finishing up, and he set the tray on the counter.

"Yes, I got your note . . . uh-huh . . . yes, he's already checked in. . . ."

There was a long pause as she listened, and when she spoke again, Paul heard her voice drop. "It's been on the news all

day. . . . From what I hear, it's supposed
to be big. . . . Oh, okay . . . under the
house? . . . Yeah, I suppose I can do
that . . . I mean, how hard can it be,
right? . . . You're   welcome. . . . Enjoy
the wedding. . . . Good-bye."

Paul was putting his cup in the sink
when she turned around.

"You didn't have to bring that in," she
said.

"I know, but I was coming this way
anyway. I wanted to find out what we
were having for dinner."

"Are you getting hungry?"

Paul turned on the faucet. "A little. But
we can wait if you'd rather."

"No, I'm getting hungry, too." Then,
seeing what he was about to do, she
added: "Here, let me do that. You're
the guest."

Paul moved aside for her as Adrienne
joined him near the sink. She rinsed the
cups and pot as she spoke.

"Your choices tonight are chicken,
steak, or pasta with a cream sauce. I can

make whichever one you want, but just realize that what you don't eat today, you'll probably eat tomorrow. I can't guarantee we'll find a store open this weekend."

"Anything's fine. You pick."

"Chicken? It's already thawed."

"Sure."

"And I was thinking of having potatoes and green beans on the side."

"Sounds great."

She dried her hands with a paper towel, then reached for the apron that was slung over the handle of the oven. Slipping it over her sweater, she went on.

"Are you interested in salad, too?"

"If you're having one. But if not, that's okay, too."

She smiled. "Boy, you weren't kidding when you said you weren't picky."

"My motto is that as long as I don't have to cook it, I'll eat just about anything."

"You don't like to cook?"

"Never really had to. Martha—my

ex—was always trying out new recipes. And since she left, I've pretty much been eating out every night."

"Well, try not to hold me to restaurant standards. I can cook, but I'm not a chef. As a general rule, my sons are more interested in quantity, not originality."

"I'm sure it'll be fine. I'd be glad to give you a hand, though."

She glanced at him, surprised by the offer. "Only if you want to. If you'd rather relax upstairs or read, I can let you know when it's ready."

He shook his head. "I didn't bring anything to read, and if I lie down now, I won't be able to sleep tonight."

She hesitated, considering his offer before finally motioning toward the door on the far side of the kitchen. "Well . . . thanks. You can start by peeling the potatoes. They're in the pantry right over there, second shelf, next to the rice."

Paul headed for the pantry. As she opened the refrigerator to get the chicken out, she watched him from the corner of her eye, thinking it was both nice—and a little disconcerting—to know that he'd be helping her in the kitchen. There was an implied familiarity to it that left her slightly off balance.

"Is there anything to drink?" Paul called out from behind her. "In the refrigerator, I mean?"

Adrienne pushed aside a few items before looking on the bottom shelf. There were three bottles held in place by a jar of pickles.

"Do you like wine?"

"What kind is it?"

She set the chicken on the counter, then pulled one of the bottles out.

"It's a pinot grigio. Is that okay?"

"I've never tried it. I usually go with a chardonnay. Have you?"

"No."

He crossed the kitchen, carrying the potatoes. After setting them on the counter, he reached for the wine. Adrienne saw him study the label for a moment before looking up.

"Sounds okay. Says it's got hints of apples and oranges, so how bad can it be? Do you know where I might find a corkscrew?"

"I think I saw one in one of the drawers around here. Let me check."

Adrienne opened the drawer below the utensils, then the one next to it, without luck. Finally she located it, and as she handed it to him, her fingers brushed his. With a few quick moves, he removed the cork and set it off to the side. Hanging below the cabinet near the oven were glasses, and Paul moved toward them. He took one out and hesitated.

"Would you like me to pour you a glass?"

"Why not?" she said, still feeling the sensation of his touch.

Paul poured two glasses and brought one over. He smelled the wine, then took a sip as Adrienne did the same. As the flavor lingered on the back of her throat, she found herself still trying to make sense of things.

"What do you think?" he asked.

"It's good."

"That's what I think." He swirled the wine in his glass. "Actually, it's better than I thought it would be. I'll have to remember this."

Adrienne felt the sudden urge to retreat and took a small step backward. "Let me get started on the chicken."

"I guess that's my signal to get to work."

As Adrienne found the roasting pan beneath the oven, Paul set his glass on the counter and moved to the sink. After turning on the faucet, he soaped and scrubbed his hands. She noticed that he washed both the oy1 front and the back, then cleaned his fingers individually. She turned on the oven, set it to the temperature she wanted, and heard the gas click to life.

"Is there a peeler handy?" he asked.

"I couldn't find one earlier, so I think you'll have to use a paring knife. Is that okay?"

Paul laughed under his breath. "I think I can handle it. I'm a surgeon," he said.

As soon as he said the words, it all clicked: the lines on his face, the intensity of his gaze, the way he'd washed his hands. She wondered why she hadn't thought of it before. Paul moved beside her and reached for the potatoes, starting to clean them.

"You practiced in Raleigh?" she asked.

"I used to. I sold my practice last month."

"You retired?"

"In a way. Actually, I'm heading off to join my son."

"In Ecuador?"

"If he'd asked, I would have recommended the south of France, but I doubt he would have listened to me."

She smiled. "Do they ever?"

"No. But then again, I didn't listen to my father, either. It's all part of growing up, I guess."

For a moment, neither of them said

anything. Adrienne added assorted spices to the chicken. Paul started to peel, his hands moving efficiently.

"I take it Jean's worried about the storm," he commented.

She glanced at him. "How could you tell?"

"Just the way you got quiet on the phone. I figured she was telling you what needed to be done to get the house ready."

"You're pretty perceptive."

"Is it going to be hard? I mean, I'd be glad to help if you need it."

"Be careful—I just might take you up on that. My ex-husband was the one who was good with a hammer, not me. And to be honest, he wasn't all that good, either."

"It's an overrated skill, I've always believed." He set the first potato on the chopping block and reached for the second one. "If you don't mind my asking, how long have you been divorced?"

She wasn't sure she wanted to talk about this, but surprised herself by answering anyway.

"Three years. But he'd been gone for a year before that."

"Do the kids live with you?"

"Most of the time. Right now, they're on school break, so they're visiting their father. How long's it been for you?"

"Just a few months. It was final last October. But she was gone for a year before that, too."

"She was the one who left?"

Paul nodded. "Yeah, but it was more my fault than hers. I was hardly home, and she just got fed up with it. If I were her, I probably would have done the same thing."

Adrienne mused over his answer, thinking that the man standing next to her seemed nothing like the man he just described. "What kind of surgery did you do?"

After he told her, she looked up. Paul went on, as if anticipating questions.

"I got into it because I liked to see the obvious results of what I was doing, and there was a lot of satisfaction in knowing that I was helping people. In the beginning, it was mainly reconstructive work after accidents, or birth defects, things like that. But in the last few years, it's changed. Now, people come in for plastic surgery. I've done more nose jobs in the past six months than I ever imagined possible."

"What do I need done?" she asked playfully.

He shook his head. "Nothing at all."

"Seriously."

"I am being serious. I wouldn't change a thing."

"Really?"

He raised two fingers. "Scout's honor."

"Were you ever a Scout?"

"No."

She laughed but felt her cheeks redden anyway. "Well, thank you."

"You're welcome."

When the chicken was ready, Adrienne

put it into the oven and set the timer, then washed her hands again. Paul rinsed the potatoes and left them near the sink.

"What next?"

"There are tomatoes and cucumbers for the salad in the refrigerator."

Paul moved around her, opened the door, and found them. Adrienne could smell his cologne lingering in the small space between them.

"What was it like growing up in Rocky Mount?" he asked.

Adrienne wasn't quite sure what to say at first, but after a few minutes, she settled into the type of chitchat that was both familiar and comfortable. She shared stories of her father and mother, she mentioned the horse her father had bought for her when she was twelve, and she recalled the hours they'd spent taking care of it together and how it had taught her more about responsibility than anything she'd done to that point. Her college years were described with fondness, and she mentioned how she'd bumped into Jack at a fraternity party during her senior year. They'd dated for two years, and when she took her vows, she'd done so with the belief it would last forever. She'd trailed off then, shaking her head slightly, and turned the topic to her children, not wanting to dwell on the divorce.

As she spoke, Paul threw the salad together, topping it with the croutons she'd bought earlier, asking questions every so often, just enough to let her know he was interested in what she was saying. The animation on her face as she talked about her father and her children made him smile.

Dusk was settling in, and shadows began stretching across the room. Adrienne set the table as Paul added some more wine to both their glasses. When the meal was ready, they took their places at the table.

Over dinner, it was Paul who did most of the talking. Paul told her about his childhood on the farm, described the ordeals of medical school and the time he spent running cross-country, and spoke about some of his earlier visits to the Outer Banks. When he shared memories of his father, Adrienne considered telling him what was going on with hers, but at the last minute she held back. Jack and Martha were mentioned only in passing; so was Mark. For the most part, their conversation touched only on the surface of things, and for the time being, neither one of them was ready to go any deeper than that.

By the time they finished dinner, the wind had slowed to a breeze and the clouds balled together in the calm before the storm. Paul brought the dishes to the sink as Adrienne stored the leftovers in the refrigerator. The wine bottle was empty, the tide was coming in, and the first images of lightning began to register on the distant horizon, making the world outside flash, as if someone were taking photographs in hopes of remembering this night forever.

Eight

———✦———

After helping her with the dishes, Paul nodded toward the back door.

"Would you like to join me for a stroll on the beach?" he asked. "It looks like a nice night."

"Isn't it getting cold?"

"I'm sure it is, but I have the feeling it'll be the last chance we get for a couple of days."

Adrienne glanced out the window. She should stay and finish cleaning up the rest of the kitchen, but that could wait, right?

"Sure," she agreed, "just let me get a jacket."

Adrienne's room was located off the

kitchen, in a room that Jean had added on a dozen years ago. It was larger than the other rooms in the house and had a bathroom that had been designed around a large Jacuzzi bathtub. Jean took baths regularly, and whenever Adrienne had called her when her spirits were low, it was always the remedy that Jean recommended to make herself feel better. "What you need is a long, hot, relaxing bath," she'd say, oblivious to the fact that there were three kids in the house who monopolized the bathrooms and that Adrienne's schedule didn't allow for much free time.

From the closet, Adrienne retrieved her jacket, then grabbed her scarf. Wrapping it around her neck, she glanced at the clock and was amazed at how quickly the hours had seemed to pass. By the time she'd returned to the kitchen, Paul was waiting for her with his coat on.

"You ready?" he asked.

She folded up the collar on her jacket.

"Let's go. But I have to warn you, I'm not a real big fan of cold weather. My southern blood's a little thin."

"We won't be out long. I promise."

He smiled as they stepped outside, and Adrienne flipped the light switch that illuminated the steps. Walking side by side, they headed over the low dune, toward the compact sand near the water's edge.

There was an exotic beauty to the evening; the air was crisp and fresh, and the flavor of salt hung in the mist. On the horizon, lightning was flickering in steady rhythm, making the clouds blink. As she glanced in that direction, she noticed that Paul was watching the sky as well. His eyes, she thought, seemed to register everything.

"Have you ever seen that before? Lightning like that?" he asked.

"Not in the winter. In the summer, it happens every now and then."

"It's from the fronts coming together. I saw it start up when we were having dinner, and it makes me think this storm is going to be bigger than they're predicting."

"I hope you're wrong."

"I might be."

"But you doubt it."

He shrugged. "Let's just say had I known it was coming, I would have tried to reschedule."

"Why?"

"I'm not a big fan of storms anymore. Do you remember Hurricane Hazel? In 1954?"

"Sure, but I was kind of young then. I was more excited than scared when we lost power at the house. And Rocky Mount wasn't hit that hard, or at least our neighborhood wasn't."

"You're lucky. I was twenty-one at the time and I was at Duke. When we heard it was coming, a few of the guys on the cross-country team thought it would be a good bonding experience if we went down to Wrightsville Beach to have a hurricane party. I didn't want to go, but since I was the captain, they sort of guilted me into it."

"Isn't that where it came ashore?"

"Not exactly, but it was close enough. By the time we got there, most of the people had evacuated the island, but we were young and stupid and made our way over anyway. At first, it was kind of fun. We kept taking turns trying to lean into the wind and keep our balance, thinking the whole thing was great and wondering why everyone had been making such a big deal about it. After a few hours, though, the wind was too strong for games and the rain was coming down in sheets, so we decided to head back to Durham. But we couldn't get off the island. They'd closed the bridges once the wind topped fifty miles an hour, and we were stuck. And the storm kept getting worse. By two A.M., it was like a war zone. Trees were toppling over, roofs were tearing off, and everywhere you looked, something that could kill us was flying past the windows of the car. And it was louder than you could imagine. Rain was just pounding the car and the storm surge hit. It was high tide and a full moon to boot, and the biggest waves I'd ever seen were coming in, one right after the next. Luckily, we were far enough from the beach, but we watched four homes wash away that night. And then, when we didn't think it could get any worse, power lines started snapping. We watched the transformers explode one right after the next, and one of the lines landed near the car. It whipped in the wind the rest of the night. It was so close we could see the sparks, and there were times when it nearly hit the car. Other than praying, I don't think any of us said a single word to each other the rest of the night. It was the dumbest thing I ever did."

Adrienne hadn't taken her eyes from him as he spoke.

"You're lucky you lived."

"I know."

On the beach, the violence of the waves had caused foam to form that looked like soap bubbles in a child's bath.

"I've never told that story before," Paul finally added. "To anyone, I mean."

"Why not?"

"Because it wasn't . . . *me,* somehow. I'd never done anything risky like that before, and I never did anything like it afterward. It's almost like it happened to someone else. You'd have to know me to understand. I was the kind of guy who wouldn't go out on Friday nights so that I wouldn't fall behind in my studies."

She laughed. "I doubt that."

"It's true. I didn't."

As they walked the hard-packed sand, Adrienne glanced at the homes behind the dunes. No other lights were on, and in the shadows, Rodanthe struck her as a ghost town.

"Do you mind if I tell you something?" she asked. "I mean, I don't want you to take it the wrong way."

"I won't."

They took a few steps as Adrienne wrestled with her words.

"Well . . . it's just that when you talk about yourself, it's almost like you're talking about someone else. You say you used to work too much, but people like that don't sell their practice to head off to Ecuador. You say you didn't do crazy things, but then you tell me a story in which you did. I'm just trying to figure it out."

Paul hesitated. He didn't have to explain himself, not to her, not to anyone, but as he walked on under the flickering sky on a cold January evening, he suddenly realized that he wanted her to know him—really know him, in all his contradictions.

"You're right," he began, "because I am talking about two people. I used to be Paul Flanner the hard-driving kid who grew up to be a surgeon. The guy who worked all the time. Or Paul

Flanner the husband and father with the big house in Raleigh. But these days, I'm not any of those things. Right now, I'm just trying to figure out who Paul Flanner really is, and to be honest, I'm beginning to wonder if I'll ever find the answer."

"I think everyone feels that way sometimes. But not many people would be inspired to move to Ecuador as a result."

"Is that why you think I'm going?"

They walked in silence for a few steps before Adrienne looked at him. "No," she said, "my guess is that you're going so you can get to know your son."

Adrienne saw the surprise on his face.

"It wasn't that hard to figure out," she said. "You hardly mentioned him all night. But if you think it'll help, then I'm glad you're going."

He smiled. "Well, you're the first. Even Mark wasn't too thrilled when I let him know."

"He'll get over it."

"You think so?"

"I hope so. That's what I tell myself when I'm having trouble with my kids."

Paul gave a short laugh and motioned over his shoulder. "You want to head back?" he asked.

"I was hoping you'd say that. My ears are getting cold."

They circled back, following their own footprints in the sand. Though the moon wasn't visible, the clouds above were shining silver. In the distance, they heard the first rumbling of thunder.

"What was your ex-husband like?"

"Jack?" She hesitated, wondering whether to try to change the subject, then decided it didn't matter. Who was he going to tell? "Unlike you," she finally said, "Jack thinks he found himself already. It just happened to be with someone else while we were married."

"I'm sorry."

"So am I. Or I was, anyway. Now it's just one of those things. I try not to think about it."

Paul remembered the tears he'd seen earlier. "Does that work?"

"No, but I keep trying. I mean, what else can I do?"

"You could always go to Ecuador."

She rolled her eyes. "Yeah, wouldn't that be nice? I could come home and say something like 'Sorry, kids, you're on your own. Mom's taking off for a while.'" She shook her head. "No, for the time being, I'm kind of stuck. At least until they're all in college. Right now, they need as much stability as they can get."

"Sounds like you're a good mother."

"I try. My kids don't always think so, though."

"Look at it this way—when they have their own kids, you can get your revenge."

"Oh, I plan on it. I've already been practicing. How about some potato chips before dinner? No, of course you don't have to clean your room. Sure you can stay up late. . . ."

Paul smiled again, thinking how much

he was enjoying the conversation. Enjoying her. In the silver light of the approaching storm, she looked beautiful, and he wondered how her husband could have left her.

They made their way back to the house slowly, both of them lost in thought, taking in the sounds and sights, neither feeling the need to speak.

There was comfort in that, Adrienne thought. Too many people seemed to believe that silence was a void that needed to be filled, even if nothing important was said. She'd experienced enough of that at the endless circuit of cocktail parties that she'd once attended with Jack. Her favorite moments then had been when she'd been able to slip away unobserved and spend a few minutes on a secluded porch. Sometimes there would be someone else out there, someone she didn't know, but when they saw each other, each would nod, as if making a secret pact. *No questions, no small talk . . . agreed.*

Here, on the beach, the feeling returned. The night felt refreshing, the
breeze lifting her hair and burnishing her
skin. Shadows spread out before her on
the sand, moving and shifting, forming
into almost recognizable images, then
vanishing from sight. The ocean was a
swirl of liquid coal. Paul, she knew, was
absorbing all those things as well; he also
seemed to realize that talking now would
somehow ruin it all.

They walked on in companionable silence, Adrienne more certain with every
step that she wanted to spend more time
with him. But that wasn't so odd, was it?
He was lonely and so was she, solitary
travelers enjoying a deserted stretch of
sand in an oceanside village called
Rodanthe.

When they reached the house, they
stepped inside the kitchen and slipped off
their jackets. Adrienne hung hers on the

coat rack beside the door along with her scarf; Paul hung his beside it.

Adrienne brought her hands together and blew through them, seeing Paul look toward the clock, then around the kitchen, as if wondering whether he should call it a night.

"How about something warm to drink?" she offered quickly. "I can brew a fresh pot of decaf."

"Do you have any tea?" he asked.

"I think I saw some earlier. Let me check."

She crossed the kitchen, opened the cupboard near the sink, then moved assorted goods to the side, liking the fact that they'd have a bit more time together. A box of Earl Grey was on the second shelf, and when she turned around to show it to him, Paul nodded with a smile. She moved around him to get the kettle, then added water, conscious of how close they were standing to each other. When it whistled, she poured two cups and they went to the sitting room.

They took their places in the rockers again, though the room had changed now that the sun had dropped. If possible, it seemed quieter, more intimate in the darkness.

As they drank their tea, they talked for another hour about this and that, the easy conversation of casual friends. In time, though, as the evening was winding down, Adrienne found herself confiding in him about her father and the fears she had for the future.

Paul had heard similar scenarios before; as a doctor, he encountered such stories regularly. But until that moment, they'd been just that: stories. His parents were gone, and Martha's parents were alive and well and living in Florida; but he could tell by Adrienne's expression that her dilemma was something he was glad he wouldn't have to face.

"Is there something I can do?" he offered. "I know a lot of specialists who could review his chart and see if there's a way to help him."

"Thank you for the offer, but no, I've done all that. The last stroke really set him back. Even if there was something that might help a little, I don't think there's any chance that he could function without round-the-clock care."

"What are you going to do?"

"I don't know. I'm hoping Jack will change his mind about coming up with additional financial support for my dad, and he might. He and my father were pretty close for a while. But if not, I guess I'll look for a full-time position so I can pay for it."

"Can't the state do anything?"

As soon as he said the words, he knew what her answer would be.

"He might be eligible for assistance, but the good places have long waiting lists, and most of them are a couple of hours away, so I wouldn't be able to see him regularly. And the not-so-good places? I couldn't do that to him."

She paused, her thoughts flashing between the past and present. "When he retired," she finally said, "they had a small party at the plant for him, and I remember thinking that he was going to miss going in every day. He'd started working there when he was fifteen, and in all the years he spent with them, he only took two sick days. I figured it out once—if you add up all the hours he spent working there, it added up to fifteen years of his life, but when I asked him about it, he said he wasn't going to miss it at all. That he had big plans now that he was finished."

Adrienne's expression softened. "What he meant was that he was planning to do the things he wanted instead of the things he had to do. Spending time with me, with the grandkids, with his books, or with friends. He deserved a few easy years after all he'd been through, and then . . ." She trailed off before meeting Paul's eyes. "You would like him if you met him. Even now."

"I'm sure I would. But would he like me?"

Adrienne smiled. "My dad likes everyone. Before his strokes, there was nothing more enjoyable to him than listening to people talk and learning what they were all about. He was endlessly patient, and because of that, people always opened up to him. Even strangers. They would tell him things they wouldn't tell anyone else because they knew he could be trusted." She hesitated. "You want to know what I remember most, though?"

Paul raised his eyebrows slightly.

"It was something he used to say to me, ever since I was a little girl. No matter how good or bad I'd done in anything, no matter if I was happy or sad, my dad would always give me a hug and tell me, 'I'm proud of you.'"

She was quiet for a moment. "I don't know what it is about those words, but they always moved me. I must have heard them a million times, but every time he said them, they left me with the feeling that he'd love me no matter what. It's funny, too, because as I got older, I used to joke with him about it. But even then, when I was getting ready to leave, he'd say it anyway, and I'd still get all mushy inside."

Paul smiled. "He sounds like a remarkable man."

"He is," she said, and sat up straighter in her chair. "And because of that, I'll work it out so he won't have to leave. It's the best place in the world for him. It's close to home, and not only is the care exceptional, but they treat him like a person there, not just a patient. He deserves a place like that, and it's the least I can do."

"He's lucky he has you as a daughter to watch out for him."

"I'm lucky, too." As she stared toward the wall, her eyes seemed to lose their focus. Then she shook her head, suddenly realizing what she'd been saying. "But listen to me going on and on. I'm sorry."

"No reason to be sorry. I'm glad you did."

With a smile, she leaned forward

slightly. "What do you miss the most about being married?"

"I take it we're changing the subject."

"I figured it was your turn to share."

"It's the least you could do?"

She shrugged. "Something along those lines. Now that I've spilled my guts, it's your turn."

Paul gave a mock sigh and gazed up at the ceiling. "Okay, what I miss." He brought his hands together. "I guess it's knowing that someone is waiting for me when I get home from work. Usually, I wouldn't be home until late, and sometimes Martha would already be in bed. But the knowledge that she was there seemed natural and reassuring, like the way things should be. How about you?"

Adrienne set her teacup on the table between them.

"The usual things. Someone to talk to, to share meals with, those quick morning kisses before either of us had brushed our teeth. But to be honest, with the kids, I'm more worried about what they're missing than what I am right now. I miss having Jack around, for their sake. I think little kids need a mom more than they need a dad, but as teenagers, they need their dads. Especially girls. I don't want my daughter thinking that men are jerks who walk out on their family, but how am I going to teach her that if her own father did it?"

"I don't know."

Adrienne shook her head. "Do men think about those things?"

"The good ones do. Like in everything else."

"How long were you married?"

"Thirty years. You?"

"Eighteen."

"Between the two of us, you'd think we'd have figured it out, huh?"

"What? The key to happily ever after? I don't think there is one anymore."

"No, I guess you're right."

From the hallway, they heard the grandfather clock beginning to chime. When it stopped, Paul rubbed the back of his neck, trying to work out the soreness from the drive. "I think I'm ready to turn in. Early day tomorrow."

"I know," she agreed, "I was just thinking the same thing."

But they didn't get up right away. Instead, they sat together for a few more minutes with the same silence they'd shared on the beach. Occasionally, he glanced toward her, but he would turn away before she caught him.

With a sigh, Adrienne got up from her chair and pointed toward his cup. "I can bring that into the kitchen. I'm going that way."

He smiled as he handed it over. "I had a good time tonight."

"So did I."

A moment later, Adrienne watched as Paul headed up the stairs before she turned away and began closing up the Inn.

In her room, she slipped out of her clothes and opened her suitcase, looking for a pair of pajamas. As she did, she caught the reflection of herself in the mirror. Not too bad, but let's be honest here—she looked her age. Paul, she thought, had been sweet when he'd said she'd needed nothing done.

It had been a long time since someone had made her feel attractive.

She put on a pair of pajamas and crawled into bed. Jean had a stack of magazines on the stand, and she browsed the articles for a few minutes before turning out the light. In the darkness, she couldn't stop thinking about the evening she'd just spent. The conversations replayed endlessly in her mind; she could see the way the corners of his mouth formed into a crooked smile whenever she'd said something he found humorous. For an hour, she tossed and turned, unable to sleep, growing frustrated, and completely unaware of the fact that in the room upstairs, Paul Flanner was doing exactly the same thing.

Nine

———◆———

Despite closing the shutters and drapes to keep out the morning light, Paul woke with Friday's dawn, and he spent ten minutes stretching the ache from his body.

Swinging open the shutters, he took in the morning. There was a deep haze over the water, and the skies were gunmetal gray. Cumulous clouds raced along, rolling parallel with the shore. The storm, he thought, would be here before night-fall more likely by midafternoon.

He sat on the edge of the bed as he slipped into his running gear, then added a windbreaker over the top. From the drawer, he removed an extra pair of socks and slipped them on his hands. Then, after padding down the stairs, he looked around. Adrienne wasn't up, and he felt a short stab of disappointment at not seeing her, then suddenly wondered why it mattered. He unlocked the door, and a minute later he was trudging along, letting his body warm up before he moved into a steadier pace.

From her bedroom, Adrienne heard him descend the creaking steps. Sitting up, she pushed off the covers and slipped her feet into a pair of slippers, wishing she'd at least had some coffee ready for Paul when he awoke. She wasn't sure he would have wanted any before his run, but she at could at least have made the offer.

Outside, Paul's muscles and joints were beginning to loosen and he quickened his stride. It wasn't anywhere near the pace he'd run in his twenties or thirties, but it was steady and refreshing.

Running had never been simply exercise for him. He'd reached the point where running wasn't difficult at all; it seemed to take no more energy to jog five miles than it did to read the paper. Instead, he viewed it as a form of meditation, one of the few times he could be alone.

It was a wonderful morning to run. Though it had rained during the night and he could see drops on the windshields of cars, the shower must have passed through the area quickly, because most of the roads had already dried. Tendrils of mist lingered in the dawn and moved in ghostly procession from one small home to the next. He would have liked to run on the beach since he didn't often have that opportunity, but he'd decided to use his run to find the home of Robert Torrelson instead. He ran along the highway, passing through downtown, then turned at the first corner, his eyes taking in the scene.

In his estimation, Rodanthe was exactly what it appeared to be: an old fishing village riding the water's edge, a place where modern life had been slow in coming. Every home was made of wood, and though some were in better repair than others, with small, well-tended yards and a thin patch of dirt where bulbs would blossom in the spring, he could see evidence of the harshness of coastal life everywhere he looked. Even homes that were no more than a dozen years old were decaying. Fences and mailboxes had small holes eaten away by the weather, paint had peeled, tin roofs were streaked with long, wide rows of rust. Scattered in the front yards were various items of everyday life in this part of the world: skiffs and broken boat engines, fishing nets used as decoration, ropes and chains used to keep strangers at bay.

Some homes were no more than shacks, and the walls seemed precariously balanced, as if the next strong wind might topple them over. In some cases, the front porches were sagging and had been propped up by an assortment of utilitarian items to keep them from giving way completely: concrete blocks or stacked bricks; two-by-fours that protruded from below like short chopsticks.

But there was activity here, even in the dawn, even in those homes that looked abandoned. As he ran, he saw smoke billowing from chimneys and watched men and women covering windows with plywood. The sound of hammering had begun to fill the air.

He turned at the next block, checked the street sign, and ran on. A few minutes later, he turned onto the street where Robert Torrelson lived. Robert Torrelson, he knew, lived at number thirty-four.

He passed number eighteen, then twenty, and raised his eyes, looking ahead. A couple of the neighbors stopped their work and watched him as he jogged by, their eyes wary. A moment later, he reached Robert Torrelson's home, trying not to be obvious as he glanced toward it.

It was a home like most of the others along the street: not exactly well tended, but not a shack, either. Rather, it was somewhere in between—a sort of stalemate between man and nature in their battle over the house. At least half a century old, the house was single storied with a tin roof; without gutters to divert runoff, the rain of a thousand storms had streaked the white paint with gray. On the porch were two weathered rockers angled toward each other. Around the windows, he could see a lone strand of Christmas lights.

Toward the back of the property was a small outbuilding with the front doors propped open. Inside were two workbenches, covered with nets and fishing rods, chests and tools. Two large grappling hooks were leaning against the wall, and he could see a yellow rain slicker hanging on a peg, just inside. From the shadows behind it, a man emerged, carrying a bucket.

The figure caught Paul off guard, and he turned away before the man could see him staring. It was too early to pay him a visit, nor did he want to do this in running clothes. Instead, he raised his chin against the breeze, turned at the next corner, and tried to find his earlier pace.

It wasn't easy. The image of the man stayed with him, making him feel sluggish, each step more difficult than the last. Despite the cold, by the time he finished, there was a thin sheen of sweat on his face.

He walked the last fifty yards to the Inn, letting his legs cool down. From the road, he could see that the light in the kitchen had been turned on.

Knowing what it meant, he smiled.

———◆———

While Paul was out, Adrienne's children had phoned and she'd spent a few minutes talking to each of them, glad they were having a good time with their father. A little while later, at the top of the hour, she called the nursing home.

Though her father couldn't answer the phone, she'd made arrangements to have Gail, one of the nurses, answer for him, and she'd picked up on the second ring.

"Right on time," Gail said. "I was just telling your father that you'd be calling any minute."

"How's he doing today?"

"He's a little tired, but other than that, he's fine. Hold on while I put the phone by his ear, okay?"

A moment later, when she heard her father's raspy breaths, Adrienne closed her eyes.

"Hi, Daddy," she started, and for several minutes she visited with him, just as she would have had she been there with him. She told him about the Inn and the beach, the storm clouds and the lightning, and though she didn't mention Paul, she wondered if her father could hear the same tremor in her voice that she could as she danced around his name.

———•———

Paul made his way up the steps, and inside, the aroma of bacon filled the air, as if welcoming him home. A moment later, Adrienne pushed through the swinging doors.

She was wearing jeans and a light blue sweater that accented the color of her eyes. In the morning light, they were almost turquoise, reminding him of crystal skies in spring.

"You were up early," she said, tucking a loose strand of hair behind her ear.

To Paul, the gesture seemed oddly sensual, and he wiped at the sweat on his brow. "Yeah, I wanted to get my run out of the way before the rest of the day starts."

"Did it go okay?"

"I've felt better, but at least it's done."

He shifted from one foot to the other. "It smells great in here, by the way."

"I started breakfast while you were out." She motioned over her shoulder. "Do you want to eat now or wait a little?"

"I'd like to shower first, if that's okay."

"It's fine. I was thinking of making grits, which take twenty minutes anyway. How do you want your eggs?"

"Scrambled?"

"I think I can manage that." She paused, liking the frankness of his stare and letting it continue for a moment longer. "Let me get the bacon before it burns," she finally said. "See you in a few?"

"Sure."

After watching her go, Paul climbed the steps to his room, shaking his head, thinking how nice she'd looked. He took off his clothes, rinsed his shirt in the sink and hung it over the curtain rod, then turned the faucet. As Adrienne had warned, it took a while before the hot water came on.

He showered, shaved, and threw on a pair of Dockers, a collared shirt, and loafers, then went to join her. In the kitchen, Adrienne had set the table and was carrying the last two bowls to the table, one with toast, the other with sliced fruit. As Paul moved around her, he caught a trace of the jasmine shampoo she'd used on her hair that morning.

"I hope you don't mind if I join you again," she said.

Paul pulled out her chair. "Not at all. In fact, I was hoping you would. Please." He motioned for her to sit.

She let him push her chair in for her, then watched him take his seat as well. "I tried to scrounge up a paper," she said, "but the rack at the general store was already empty by the time I got there."

"I'm not surprised. There were lots of people out this morning. I guess everyone's wondering how bad it's going to be today."

"It doesn't look much worse than it did yesterday."

"That's because you don't live here."

"You don't live here, either."

"No, but I've been in a big storm before. In fact, did I ever tell you about the time I was in college and went down to Wilmington . . ."

Adrienne laughed. "And you swore you never told that story."

"I guess it's coming easier now that I've broken the ice. And it's my one good story. Everything else is boring."

"I doubt that. From what you've told me, I'm thinking that your life has been anything but boring."

He smiled, unsure if she meant it as a compliment, but pleased nonetheless.

"What did Jean say had to be done today?"

Adrienne scooped out some eggs and passed the bowl toward him.

"Well, the furniture on the porches needs to be stored in the shed. The windows need to be closed and the shutters latched from the inside. Then, the hurricane guards have to be put up. Supposedly, they lock together and there are some hooks you drop in to keep them in place; after that, we brace them with two-by-fours. The wood for that is supposed to be stacked with the hurricane guards."

"She has a ladder, I hope."

"It's under the house, too."

"It doesn't sound too bad. But like I said yesterday, I'd be happy to help you with it after I get back later this morning."

She looked at him. "You sure. You don't have to do this."

"It's no bother. I don't have anything else planned, anyway. And to be honest, it would be impossible for me to sit inside while you were doing all that work. I'd feel guilty, even if I'm the guest."

"Thank you."

"No problem."

They finished serving up, poured the coffee, and started eating. Paul watched her butter a piece of toast, momentarily absorbed in her task. In the gray morning light, she was pretty, even prettier than he'd realized the day before.

"You're going to talk to that person you mentioned yesterday?"

Paul nodded. "After breakfast," he said.

"You don't sound too happy about it."

"I don't know whether to be happy or not."

"Why?"

After the briefest hesitation, he told her about Jill and Robert Torrelson—the operation, the autopsy, and all that had happened in the aftermath, including the note he'd received in the mail. When he finished, Adrienne seemed to be studying him.

"And you have no idea what he wants?"

"I assume it's something about the lawsuit."

Adrienne wasn't so sure about that, but she said nothing. Instead, she reached for her coffee.

"Well, no matter what happens, I think

you're doing the right thing. Just like you're doing with Mark."

He didn't say anything, but then, he didn't have to. The fact that she understood was more than enough.

It was all that he wanted from anyone these days, and though he'd met her only the day before, he sensed that somehow she already knew him better than most people did.

Or maybe, he thought, better than anyone.

Ten

After breakfast, Paul got into his car and fished the keys from the pocket of his coat. From the porch, Adrienne waved, as if wishing him luck. A moment later, Paul looked over his shoulder and began backing out of the drive.

He reached Torrelson's street in a few minutes; though he could have walked, he didn't know how fast the weather would deteriorate, and he didn't want to be caught in the rain. Nor did he want to feel trapped if the meeting started to go badly. Though he wasn't sure what to expect, he decided he would tell Torrelson everything that had happened with re-

gard to the operation but wouldn't spec-
ulate on what had caused her death.

He slowed the car, pulled it to the side
of the road, and switched off the engine.
After taking a moment to prepare himself, he got out and started up the walk-
way. A neighbor next door was standing
on a ladder, hammering a piece of plywood over a window. He looked over at
Paul, trying to figure out who he was.
Paul ignored the stare, and when he
reached Torrelson's door, he knocked,
then stepped back, giving himself space.

When no one came to the door, he
knocked again, this time listening for
movement inside. Nothing. He moved
to the side of the porch. Though the
doors of the outbuilding were still open,
he didn't see anyone. He considered calling out but decided against it. Instead, he
went to the trunk of his car and opened
it. From the medical kit, he pulled out a
pen and tore a scrap of paper from one of
the notebooks he'd stuffed inside.

He wrote his name and where he was

staying, as well as a brief message saying that he would be in town until Tuesday morning if Robert still wanted to talk to him. Then, folding the paper, he brought the note to the front porch and wedged it into the frame, making sure it wouldn't blow away. He was heading back to the car, feeling both disappointed and relieved, when he heard a voice behind him.

"Can I help you?"

When Paul turned, he didn't recognize the man standing near the house. Though he couldn't recall what Robert Torrelson looked like—his face was one of thousands—he knew he'd never seen this person before. He was a young man in his thirties or so, gaunt with thinning black hair, dressed in a sweatshirt and work jeans. He was staring at Paul with the same wariness the neighbor had shown him earlier when he'd first pulled up.

Paul cleared his throat. "Yes," he said. "I was looking for Robert Torrelson. Is this the right place?"

The young man nodded without changing his expression. "Yeah, he lives here. That's my dad."

"Is he in?"

"You with the bank?"

Paul shook his head. "No. My name is Paul Flanner."

It was a moment before the young man recognized the name. His eyes narrowed.

"The doctor?"

Paul nodded. "Your father sent me a letter saying he wanted to speak to me."

"What for?"

"I don't know."

"He didn't tell me about no letter." As he spoke, the muscles in his jaw began to clench.

"Can you tell him I'm here?"

The young man hooked his thumb into his belt. "He's not in."

As he said it, his eyes flashed to the house, and Paul wondered if he was telling the truth.

"Will you at least tell him I came by? I

left a note on the door telling him where he can reach me."

"He doesn't want to talk to you."

Paul dropped his gaze, then looked up again.

"I think that's for him to decide, don't you?" he said.

"Who the hell do you think you are? You think you can come here and try to talk your way out of what you did? Like it was just some mistake or something?"

Paul said nothing. Sensing his hesitation, the young man took a step toward him and went on, his voice rising.

"Just get the hell out of here! I don't want you around here anymore, and my dad doesn't, either!"

"Fine . . . okay. . . ."

The young man reached for a nearby shovel and Paul raised his hands, backing away.

"I'm going. . . ."

He turned and started toward the car.

"And don't come back," the young

man shouted. "Don't you think you've done enough already? My mother's dead because of you!"

Paul flinched at the words, feeling their sting, then got in the car. After starting the engine, he pulled away without looking back.

He didn't see the neighbor come down from the ladder to speak with the young man; he didn't see the young man throw the shovel. He didn't see the living room curtain fall back into place inside the house.

Nor did he see the front door open or the wrinkled hand that retrieved the note after it had fallen to the porch.

———

Minutes later, Adrienne was listening to Paul as he recounted what had happened. They were in the kitchen, and Paul was leaning against the counter, his arms crossed as he gazed out the window. His expression was blank, withdrawn; he looked far more tired than he had earlier in the morning. When he finished, Adrienne's face showed a mixture of sympathy and concern.

"At least you tried," she said.

"A lot of good that did, huh?"

"Maybe he didn't know about his father's letter."

Paul shook his head. "It's not just that. It goes back to the whole reason I came here. I wanted to see if I could fix it somehow or at least make it understandable, but I'm not even going to get the chance."

"That's not your fault."

"Then why does it feel that way?"

In the silence that followed, Adrienne could hear the ticking of the heater.

"Because you care. Because you've changed."

"Nothing's changed. They still think I killed her." He sighed. "Can you imagine how it feels to know that someone believes that about you?"

"No," she admitted, "I can't. I've never had to go through something like that."

Paul nodded, looking drawn.

Adrienne watched to see if his expression would change, and when it didn't, she surprised herself by moving toward him and reaching for his hand. It was stiff at first, but he relaxed and she felt his fingers curl into hers.

"As hard as it is to accept, and no matter what anyone says," she said carefully, "you have to understand that even if you had talked to the father this morning, you probably wouldn't have changed his son's mind. He's hurting, and it's easier to blame someone like you than to accept the fact that his mother's time had come. And no matter how you think it went, you did do something important by going there this morning."

"What's that?"

"You listened to what the son had to say. Even though he's wrong, you gave him the chance to tell you how he feels. You let him get it off his chest, and in the end, that's probably what the father wanted all along. Since he knows the case isn't going to make it to court, he wanted you to hear his side of the story in person. To know how they feel."

Paul laughed grimly. "That makes me feel a whole lot better."

Adrienne squeezed his hand. "What did you expect would happen? That they'd listen to what you had to say and accept it after a few minutes? After hiring a lawyer and continuing the suit, even when they knew they didn't have a chance? After hearing what all the other doctors had said? They wanted you to come so *you* could listen to *them*. Not the other way around."

Paul said nothing, but deep down he knew she was right. Why, though, hadn't he realized it before?

"I know it wasn't easy to hear," she went on, "and I know they're wrong and it isn't fair to blame what happened on you. But you gave them something important today, and more than that, it was something you didn't have to do. You can be proud of that."

"None of what happened surprised you, did it?"

"Not really."

"Did you know that this morning? When I first told you about them?"

"I wasn't sure, but I thought it might go like this."

A brief smile flickered across his face. "You're something, you know that?"

"Is that a good thing or a bad thing?"

He squeezed her hand, thinking that he liked the way it felt in his. It felt natural, almost as if he'd been holding it for years.

"It's a great thing," he said.

He turned to face her, smiling gently, and Adrienne suddenly realized that he was thinking of kissing her. Though part of her longed for just that, the rational side suddenly reminded her that it was Friday. They'd met the day before, and he'd be leaving soon. And so would she. Besides, this wasn't really her, was it? This wasn't the real Adrienne—the worried mom and daughter, or the wife who'd been left for another woman, or the lady who sorted books at the library. This weekend she was someone different, someone she barely recognized. Her time here had been dreamlike, and though dreams were pleasant, she reminded herself that they were just that and nothing more.

She took a small step backward. When she released his hand, she saw a flash of disappointment in his eyes, but it vanished as he looked off to the side.

She smiled, forcing herself to keep her voice steady.

"Are you still up for helping me with the house? Before the weather sets in, I mean?"

"Sure." Paul nodded. "Just let me throw on some work clothes."

"You've got time. I've got to run up to the store first, anyway. I forgot to get ice and a cooler so I can keep some food handy in case the power goes out."

"Okay."

She paused. "You gonna be all right?"

"I'll be fine."

She waited as if to make sure she believed him, then turned away. Yes, she told herself, she'd done the right thing. She was right to have turned away, she was right to have let go of his hand.

Yet as she slipped out the door, she couldn't escape the feeling that she'd turned away from the chance to find a piece of happiness she'd been missing for far too long.

Paul was upstairs when he heard Adrienne's car start up. Turning toward the window, he watched the waves crashing in, trying to make sense of what had just happened. A few minutes ago, when he'd looked at her, he'd felt a flash of something special, but just as quickly as it had come, it was gone, and the look on her face told him why.

He could understand Adrienne's reservations—they all lived in a world defined by limits, after all, and those didn't always allow for spontaneity, for impulsive attempts to live in the moment. He knew that was what allowed order to prevail in the course of one's life, yet his actions in recent months had been an attempt to defy those limits, to reject the order that he had embraced for so long.

It wasn't fair of him to expect the same thing of her. She was in a different place; her life had responsibilities, and as she'd made clear to him yesterday, those responsibilities required stability and predictability. He'd been the same way once, and though he was now in the position to live by different rules, Adrienne, he realized, wasn't.

Nonetheless, something had changed in the short time he'd been here. He wasn't sure when it had happened. It might have been yesterday when they were walking on the beach, or when she'd first told him about her father, or even this morning when they had eaten together in the soft light of the kitchen. Or maybe it happened when he found himself holding her hand and standing close, wanting nothing more than to gently press his lips against hers.

It didn't matter. All he knew for sure was that he was beginning to fall for a woman named Adrienne, who was watching the Inn for a friend in a tiny coastal town in North Carolina.

Eleven

——◆◆◆◆——

Robert Torrelson sat at the aging roll-top desk in his living room, listening as his son boarded up the windows at the back of the house. In his hand was the note from Paul Flanner and he was absently folding and unfolding it, still wondering at the fact that he had come.

He hadn't expected it. Though he'd written with the request, he'd been sure that Paul Flanner would ignore it. Flanner was a high-powered doctor in the city, represented by attorneys who wore flashy ties and fancy belts, and none of them had seemed to give a damn about him or his family for over a year now. Rich city folk were like that; as for him, he was glad that he'd never had to live near people who pushed paper for a living and weren't comfortable if the temperature at work wasn't exactly seventy-two degrees. Nor did he like dealing with people who thought they were better than others because they had better schooling or more money or a bigger house. Paul Flanner, when he'd met him after the surgery, had struck him as that type of person. He was stiff and distant, and though he'd explained himself, the clipped way he'd spoken the words had left Robert with the feeling that he wouldn't lose a minute's sleep because of what had happened.

And that wasn't right.

Robert had lived a life with different values, values that had been honored by his father and grandfather and their grandfather before that. He could trace his family's roots in the Outer Banks back nearly two hundred years. Generation after generation, they'd fished the waters of Pamlico Sound since the times when the fish were so plentiful that a person could cast a single net and pull in enough fish to fill the bow. But all that had changed. Now there were quotas and regulations and licenses and big companies, all chasing fewer fish than there'd ever been. These days, when Robert went down to the boat, half the time he considered himself lucky if he caught enough to pay for the gas he'd needed.

Robert Torrelson was sixty-seven but looked ten years older. His face was weathered and stained, and his body was slowly losing the battle with time. There was a long scar that ran from his left eye to his ear. His hands ached with arthritis, and the ring finger on his right hand was missing from the time he'd got it caught in a winch while dragging in the nets.

But Jill hadn't cared about any of those things. And now Jill was gone.

On the desk was a picture of her, and Robert still found himself staring at it whenever he was alone in the room. He missed everything about her; he missed the way she rubbed his shoulders after he came in on cold winter evenings, he missed the way they used to sit together and listen to music on the radio while they sat on the porch out back, he missed the way she smelled after dabbing her chest with powder, an odor that was simple and clean, fresh like a newborn.

Paul Flanner had taken all that away from him. Jill, he knew, would still have been with him had she never gone to the hospital that day.

His son had had his turn. And now the time had come for his.

———◦———

Adrienne made the short drive to town and pulled into the small gravel parking lot of the general store, breathing a sigh of relief to find that it was still open.

There were three cars out front parked haphazardly, each coated with a thin layer of salt. A couple of older men wearing baseball hats were standing out front, smoking and drinking coffee. They watched Adrienne as she got out of the car, and they stopped speaking; as she passed them on her way into the store, they nodded a greeting.

The store was typical of those in rural areas: a scuffed wooden floor, ceiling fans, shelves with thousands of various items packed close together. Near the register was a small barrel offering dill pickles for sale; next to that was another barrel containing roasted peanuts. In the rear was a small grill offering fresh cooked burgers and fish sandwiches, and though no one was behind the counter, the odor of fried food lingered in the air.

The ice machine was in the far rear corner, next to the refrigerated compartments containing beer and soda, and Adrienne headed that way. As she reached for the handle of the ice machine door, she caught a glimpse of herself in the mirrored door panel. She stopped for a moment, as if seeing herself through different eyes.

How long had it been, she wondered, since someone had found her attractive? Or someone she'd just met had wanted to kiss her? If someone had asked her those questions before she'd come here, she would have answered that neither of those things had happened since the day Jack had moved out. But that wasn't exactly true, was it? Not like this, anyway. Jack had been her husband, not a stranger, and since they'd dated for two years before they walked down the aisle, it was closer to twenty-three years since she'd encountered something like this.

Of course, had Jack not left, she could have lived with that knowledge and never thought twice about it; but here and now, she found that impossible. More than half her life had passed without the interest of an attractive man, and no matter how much she wanted to convince herself that her reasons for turning away had been based on common sense, she couldn't help but think that being out of practice for twenty-three years had something to do with it as well.

She was drawn to Paul, she couldn't deny that. It wasn't just that he was handsome and interesting, or even charming in his own quiet way. Nor was it just the fact that he'd made her feel desirable. No, it was his genuine desire to change—to be a better person than he had been—that she found most compelling. She'd known people like him before in her life—like physicians, attorneys were often notorious workaholics—but she had yet to come across someone who'd not only made the decision to change the rules that he'd always lived by, but was doing so in a way that most people would be terrified to contemplate.

There was, she decided, something noble in that. He wanted to fix the flaws he recognized in himself, he wanted to forge a relationship with his estranged son, he had come here because a stranger seeking redress from him had sent a note requesting it.

What kind of person did those things? What kind of strength would that take? Or courage? More than she had, she thought. More than anyone she knew, and as much as she wanted to deny it, she was gratified that someone like him had found her attractive.

As she reflected on these things, Adrienne grabbed the last two bags of ice and a Styrofoam cooler and carried it all to the register. After paying, she left the store and headed for the car. One of the elderly men was still sitting on the porch as she left, and as she nodded to him, she wore the odd expression of someone who had attended a wedding and a funeral on exactly the same day.

In her brief absence the sky had grown darker, and the wind cut past her as she stepped out of the car. It had begun to whistle as it moved around the Inn, sounding almost ghostlike, a spectral flute playing a single note. Clouds swirled and banded together, shifting in clumps as they passed overhead. The ocean was a sea of whitetips, and the waves were rolling heavily past the high-water mark from the day before.

As she was reaching for the ice, Adrienne saw Paul come out from behind the gate.

"Did you get started without me?" she called out.

"No, not really. I was just making sure I could find everything." He motioned to the load. "Do you need a hand with that?"

Adrienne shook her head. "I've got it. It's not that heavy." She nodded toward the door. "But let me get started in there. Would you mind if I went into your room to close up the shutters?"

"No, go ahead. I don't mind."

Inside, Adrienne set the cooler next to

the refrigerator, cut open the bags of ice with a steak knife, and poured them in. She pulled out some cheese, the fruit that had been left over from breakfast, and the chicken from the night before, stacking it with the ice, thinking it wasn't a gourmet meal, but good enough in case nothing else was available. Then, noting that there was still room, she grabbed one of the bottles of wine and put it on top, feeling a forbidden thrill at the thought of sharing the wine with Paul later.

Forcing the feeling away, she spent the next few minutes making sure all the windows were closed and latching the shutters from the inside on the bottom floor. Upstairs, she took care of the empty guest rooms first, then made her way to the room where he'd slept.

After unlocking the door, she stepped in, noticing that Paul had made his own bed. His duffel bags were folded beside the chest of drawers; the clothes he'd worn earlier that morning had already been put away, and his loafers were on the floor near the wall, toes together and facing out. Her children, she thought to herself, could learn something from him about the virtues of keeping things neat in their rooms.

In his bathroom, she closed up a small window, and as she did, she spied the soap dish and brush he used to create lather lying next to his razor. Both were near the sink, next to a bottle of after-shave. Unbidden, an image came to her of him standing over the sink that morn-ing; and as she pictured him there, some instinct told her that he'd wanted her beside him.

She shook her head, feeling strangely like a teenager poking through a parent's bedroom, and headed to the window be-side his bed. As she was closing it up, she saw Paul carrying one of the rockers off the porch to store beneath the house.

He moved as if he were twenty years younger. Jack wasn't like that. Over the years, Jack had grown heavy around the midsection from one too many cocktails, and his belly tended to shimmy if he engaged in any sort of physical activity.

But Paul was different. Paul, she knew, wasn't like Jack in any way, and it was there, while upstairs in his room, that Adrienne first felt a vague sense of anxious anticipation, something akin to what a high roller might feel when hoping for a lucky roll of the dice.

Beneath the house, Paul was getting things ready.

The hurricane guards were corrugated aluminum, two and a half feet wide and six feet high, and all had been labeled with a permanent marker as to which window they protected on the house. Paul began lifting them from the stack and setting them aside, putting each group together, mentally outlining what he needed to do.

He was finishing up just as Adrienne

came back down. Thunder sounded in the distance, rumbling long and low over the water. The temperature, she noticed, was beginning to drop: "How's it going?" she asked. Her tone, she thought, was unfamiliar; like another woman was speaking the words.

"It's easier than I thought it would be," he said. "All I have to do is match up the grooves and slip them into the braces, then drop these clips in."

"What about the wood to hold it in place?"

"That's not too bad, either. The joints are already up, so all I have to do is put the two-by-fours in their supports and hammer a couple of nails. Like Jean said, it's a one-person job."

"Do you think it'll take long?"

"Maybe an hour. You can wait inside if you'd like."

"Isn't there something I can do? To help, I mean?"

"Not really. But if you'd like, you could keep me company."

Adrienne smiled, liking the invitation in his voice. "You've got yourself a deal."

For the next hour or so, Paul moved from one window to the next, slipping the guards into place as Adrienne kept him company. As he worked, he could feel Adrienne's eyes on him, and he felt the same awkwardness he'd felt after she'd let go of his hand earlier that morning.

Within a few minutes a light rain started, then it began to fall with more intensity. Adrienne moved closer to the house to keep from getting wet, but she found that it didn't help much in the swirling wind. Paul neither sped up nor slowed down; the rain and wind didn't seem to affect him at all.

Another window covered, then the next. Sliding in the guards, dropping the hooks, moving the ladder. By the time the windows were done and Paul had started on the braces, there was lightning over the water and the rain was driving hard. And still Paul worked. Each nail was sunk with four blows, coming regularly, as if he'd worked in carpentry for years.

Despite the rain, they talked; Adrienne noticed that he kept the conversation light, far from anything that could be construed the wrong way. He told her about some of the repairs he and his father had done on the farm and that he might be doing a bit of this in Ecuador as well, so that it was good to get the feel of it again.

As Adrienne listened to him talk of this and that, she could tell that Paul was giving her the space he thought she needed, that he thought she wanted. But as she watched him, she suddenly knew that keeping her distance was the furthest thing from her mind.

Everything about him made her long for something she had never known: the way he made what he was doing look easy, the shape of his hips and legs in his jeans as he stood on the ladder above her, those eyes that always reflected what he was thinking and feeling. Standing in the pouring rain, she felt the pull of the person he was, and the person she realized she wanted to be.

By the time he finished, his sweatshirt and jacket were soaked and his face had paled with the cold. After storing the ladder and the tools beneath the house, he joined Adrienne on the porch. She'd run her hand through her hair, pulling it back from her face. The soft curls were gone, and so was any evidence of makeup. In their place was a natural beauty, and despite the heavy jacket she was wearing, Paul could sense the warm, feminine body beneath it.

It was then, as they were standing under the overhang, that the storm unleashed its full fury. A long, streaking lightning bolt connected sea to sky, and thunder echoed as if two cars had collided on the highway. The wind gusted, bending the limbs of trees in a single direction. Rain blew sideways, as if trying to defy gravity.

For a moment they simply watched, knowing that another minute in the rain wouldn't matter. And then, finally giving in to the possibility of what might come next, they turned and headed back into the house without a word.

Twelve

———◆———

Wet and cold, they each went to their rooms. Paul slipped out of his clothes and turned on the faucet, waiting until the steam was billowing from behind the curtain before he hopped into the shower. It took a few minutes for his body to warm up, and though he lingered far longer than usual and got dressed slowly, Adrienne hadn't reappeared by the time he went back downstairs.

With the windows covered, the house was dark, and Paul turned on the light in the sitting room before heading to the kitchen for a cup of coffee. The rain beat furiously on the hurricane guards, making the house echo with vibration. Thunder rolled continuously, sounding both close and far away at the same time, like sounds in a busy train station. Paul brought the cup of coffee back to the sitting room. Even with the lamp turned on, the blackened windows made it feel as though evening had settled in, and he moved toward the fireplace.

Paul opened the damper and added three logs, stacking them to allow for airflow, then threw in some kindling. He nosed around for the matches and found them in a wooden box on the mantel. The odor of sulfur hung in the air when he struck the first match.

The kindling was dry and caught quickly; soon he heard a sound like the crinkling of paper as the logs began to catch. Within a few minutes the oak was giving off heat, and Paul moved the rocker closer, stretching his feet toward the fire.

It was comfortable, he thought, getting up from his chair, but not quite right. He crossed the room and turned off the light.

He smiled. Better, he thought. A lot better.

———•——

In her room, Adrienne was taking her time. After they'd reentered the house, she'd decided to take Jean's advice and began filling the tub. Even when she turned off the faucet and slipped in, she could hear water running through the pipes and knew that Paul was still up-stairs showering. There was something sensual in that realization, and she let that feeling wash over her.

Two days ago, she couldn't have imag-ined this sort of thing happening to her. Nor could she have imagined that she'd be feeling this way about anyone, let alone someone she'd just met. Her life didn't allow for such things, not lately, anyway. It was easy to blame the kids or tell herself that her responsibilities didn't allow for something like this, but that wasn't completely true. It also had to do with who she'd become in the aftermath of her divorce.

Yes, she felt betrayed and angry at Jack; everyone could understand those things. But being left for someone else carried other implications, and as much as she tried not to dwell on them, there were times when she couldn't help it. Jack had rejected her, he'd rejected the life they had lived together; it was a devastating blow to her as a wife and mother, but also as a woman. Even if, as he'd claimed, he hadn't planned on falling in love with Linda and that it had just happened, it wasn't as if he simply rode the wave of emotions without making conscious decisions along the way. He had to have thought about what he was doing, he had to have considered the possibilities when he started spending time with Linda. And no matter how much he tried to soft-pedal what had happened, it was as if he'd told Adrienne not only that

Linda was better in every way, but that Adrienne wasn't even worth the time and effort it would take to fix whatever it was he thought was wrong with their relationship.

How was she supposed to react to that sort of total rejection? It was easy for others to say that it had nothing to do with her, that Jack was going through a midlife crisis, but it still had an effect on the person she thought she was. Especially as a woman. It was hard to feel sensual when you didn't feel attractive, and the ensuing three years without a date only served to underscore her feeling of inadequacy.

And how had she dealt with that feeling? She'd devoted her life to her children, her father, the house, her job, the bills. Consciously or subconsciously, she'd stopped doing those things that would give her the opportunity to think about herself. Gone were the relaxing conversations with friends on the telephone, or walks or baths, or even working in her

garden. Everything she did had a pur-
pose, and though she believed she was
keeping her life orderly in this way, she
now realized that it had been a mistake.

It hadn't helped, after all. She was busy
from the moment she woke until the
moment she went to bed, and because
she'd robbed herself of any possibility of
rewards, there was nothing to look forward to. Her daily routine was a series of
chores, and that was enough to wear
anyone down. By giving up the little
things that make life worthwhile, all
she'd done, she suddenly realized, was to
forget who she really was.

Paul, she suspected, already knew that
about her. And somehow, spending time
with him had given her the chance to realize it as well.

But this weekend wasn't simply about
recognizing the mistakes she'd made in
the past. It also had to do with the future
and how she would live from this point
on. Her past was played out; there was
nothing she could do about that, but the

future was still up for grabs, and she didn't want to live the rest of her life feeling the way she had for the last three years.

She shaved her legs and soaked in the tub for another few minutes, long enough for most of the suds to vanish and the water to start cooling. She dried off and—knowing that Jean wouldn't mind—reached for the lotion on the counter. She applied some to her legs and belly, then her breasts and arms, relishing the way it made her skin come to life.

Wrapping the towel around her, she went to her suitcase. Force of habit made her reach for jeans and a sweater, but after pulling them out, she set them aside. If I'm serious about changing the way I'm going to live, she thought, I may as well start now.

She hadn't brought much else with her, certainly nothing fancy, but she did have a pair of black pants and a white blouse that Amanda had bought her for Christmas. She'd brought those along in the vague hope that she might head out one evening, and though she wasn't going anywhere, it seemed as good a time as any to put them on.

She dried her hair with a blow dryer and curled it. Makeup came next: mascara and a dusting of blush, lipstick she'd bought at Belk's a few months back but had seldom used. Leaning toward the mirror, she added a trace of eye shadow, just enough to accent the color of her eyes, as she'd done in the early years of her marriage.

When she was ready, she tugged at the blouse until it hung just right, smiling at what she saw. It had been far too long since she'd last looked like this.

She left the bedroom, and as she passed through the kitchen, she could smell the coffee. It was what she would normally drink on a day like this, especially since it was still the afternoon, but instead of pouring a cup, she retrieved the last bottle of wine in the refrigerator, then grabbed the corkscrew and a couple of glasses, feeling worldly, as if she were finally in control.

Carrying it all to the sitting room, she saw that Paul had started the fire, and it had somehow changed the room, as though anticipating the way she was feeling. Paul's face was glowing in the flames, and though she was quiet, she knew he could sense her presence. He turned around to say something, but when he saw Adrienne, no words came out of his mouth. All he could do was stare at her.

"Too much?" she finally asked.

Paul shook his head, his eyes never leaving hers. "No . . . not at all. You look . . . beautiful."

Adrienne gave a shy smile. "Thank you," she said. Her voice was soft, almost a whisper, a voice from long ago.

They continued to stare at each other until Adrienne finally lifted the bottle slightly. "Would you like some wine?"

she asked. "I know you have coffee, but with the storm, I thought it might be nice."

Paul cleared his throat. "That sounds great. Would you like me to open the bottle?"

"Unless you like bits of cork in your wine, you'd better. I never did get the hang of those things."

When Paul rose from his chair, she handed the corkscrew to him. He opened the bottle with a series of quick movements, and Adrienne held both glasses as he poured. He set the bottle on the table and took his glass as they sat in the rockers. She noticed they were closer together than they had been the day before.

Adrienne took a sip of wine, then lowered the glass, pleased with everything: the way she looked and felt, the taste of the wine, the room itself. The flickering fire made shadows dance around them. Rain was sheeting itself against the walls.

"This is lovely," she said. "I'm glad you made a fire."

In the warming air, Paul caught a trace of the perfume she was wearing, and he shifted in his chair. "I was still cold after being outside," he said. "It seems to take a little longer every year for me to warm up."

"Even with all that exercise? And here I thought you were holding back the ravages of time."

He laughed softly. "I wish."

"You seem to be doing okay."

"You don't see me in the mornings."

"But don't you run then?"

"Before that, I mean. When I first get out of bed, I can barely move. I hobble like an old man. All that running has taken its toll over the years."

As they moved their rockers back and forth, he could see the reflection of the fire flickering in her eyes.

"Have you heard from your kids today?" he asked, trying not to stare at Adrienne too obviously.

She nodded. "They called this morning while you were out. They're getting ready for their ski trip, but wanted to touch base before they go. They're heading to Snowshoe, West Virginia, this weekend. They've been looking forward to that for a couple of months now."

"Sounds like they'll have fun."

"Yeah, Jack's good for that. Whenever they go to visit, he always has fun things planned, as if life with him would be nothing but one big party." She paused. "But that's okay. He's missing out on a lot of things, too, and I wouldn't trade places with him. You can't get these years back."

"I know," he murmured. "Believe me, I know."

She winced. "Sorry. I shouldn't have said that. . . ."

He shook his head. "It's okay. Even though you weren't talking about me, I know I've missed more than I can hope to recover. But at least I'm trying to do something about it now. I just hope it works out."

"It will."

"You think so?"

"I know so. I think you're the kind of person who accomplishes just about everything you set out to do."

"It's not that easy this time."

"Why not?"

"Mark and I aren't on very good terms these days. Actually, we're not on any terms. We haven't said more than a few words to each other in years."

She looked at him, not sure what to say. "I didn't realize it was that long," she finally offered.

"How would you? It's not something I'm proud to admit."

"What are you going to say to him? At first, I mean?"

"I have no idea." He looked at her. "Any suggestions? You seem to have a pretty good handle on the parent thing."

"Not really. I guess I'd have to know what the problem is first."

"It's a long story."

"We've got all day if you want to talk about it."

Paul took a drink, as if summoning his resolve. Then, over the next half hour, and to the accompaniment of the escalating wind and rain outside, he told her how he hadn't been around when Mark was growing up, about the argument in the restaurant, his inability to find the will to repair the rift between them. By the time he was finished, the fire was burning lower. Adrienne was quiet for a moment.

"That's a tough one," she admitted.

"I know."

"But this isn't all your fault, you know. It takes two people to keep a feud going."

"That's pretty philosophical."

"It's still true, though."

"What should I do?"

"I guess I'd say not to push too hard. I think you probably need to get to know each other before you start working on the problems between you two."

He smiled, thinking about her words. "You know, I hope your kids realize how smart their mother is."

"They don't. But I'm still hopeful."

He laughed, thinking her skin looked radiant in the gentle light. A log sparked, sending trails up the chimney. Paul added more wine to both their glasses.

"How long are you planning to stay in Ecuador?" she asked.

"I'm not sure yet. I guess that's up to Mark and how long he wants me there." He swirled his wine before looking at her. "But I'd say I'll be there at least a year. That's what I told the director, anyway."

"And then you'll come back?"

He shrugged. "Who knows. I suppose I could go anywhere. It's not like I have anything to return to in Raleigh. To be honest, I haven't thought about what I'll do when I get back. Maybe I'll take up watching bed-and-breakfasts when the owners are out of town."

She laughed. "I think you'd get pretty bored with that."

"But I'd be good if a storm was coming."

"True, but you'd have to learn to cook."

"Good point." Paul glanced toward her, his face half in shadow. "Then maybe I'll just move to Rocky Mount and figure it out from there."

At his words, Adrienne felt the blood rush to her cheeks. She shook her head and turned away.

"Don't say that."

"Say what?"

"Things you don't mean."

"What makes you think I don't mean it?"

She wouldn't meet his eyes, nor would she answer, and in the stillness of the room, he could see her chest rising and falling with her breaths. He could see a shadow of fear cross her face but didn't know if it was because she wanted him to come and was afraid he wouldn't, or didn't want him to come and was afraid he would. He reached over, resting his hand on her arm. When he spoke again his voice was soft, as if trying to comfort a small child.

"I'm sorry if that made you uncomfortable," he said, "but this weekend . . . it's like something I didn't know existed. I mean, it's been a dream. You've been a dream."

The warmth of his hand seemed to penetrate into her bones.

"I've had a wonderful time, too," she said.

"But you don't feel the same way."

She looked at him. "Paul . . . I . . ."

"No, you don't have to say anything—"

She didn't let him finish. "Yes, I do. You want an answer, and I'd like to give you one, okay?" She paused, composing her thoughts. "When Jack and I split up, it was more than just the ending of a marriage. It ended everything I'd hoped for in the future. And it ended who I was, too. I thought I wanted to move on, and I tried, but the world didn't seem all that interested in who I was anymore. Men in general weren't interested in me, and I guess I retreated into a shell. This

weekend made me realize that about myself, and I'm still coming to terms with
that."

"I'm not sure what you're trying to
tell me."

"I'm not saying this because the answer
is no. I would like to see you again.
You're charming and intelligent, and the
past two days have meant more to me
than you probably realize. But moving to
Rocky Mount? A year is a long time, and
there's no telling who either of us will be
then. Look how much you've changed
in the last six months. Can you honestly
tell me that you'll feel the same way
about all this a year from now?"

"Yes," he said, "I can."

"How can you be so sure?"

Outside, the wind was a steady gale,
howling as it blasted against the house.
The rain was hammering against the
walls and roof; the old inn creaked under
the incessant pressure.

Paul set aside his glass of wine. Staring

at Adrienne, he knew he'd never seen anyone more beautiful.

"Because," he said, "you're the only reason I'd bother to come back at all."

"Paul . . . don't . . ."

She closed her eyes, and for a moment, Paul believed he was losing her. The realization scared him more than he'd imagined possible, and he felt the last of his resistance give way. He looked up at the ceiling, then down to the floor, then focused on Adrienne again. Leaving his chair, he moved to her side. With a finger, he turned her face toward him, knowing that he was in love with her, with everything about her.

"Adrienne . . . ," he whispered, and when Adrienne finally met his gaze, she recognized the emotion in his eyes.

He couldn't say the words, but in a rush of intuitive feeling, she imagined she could hear them, and that was enough.

Because it was then, as he held her in

his unwavering gaze, that she knew she was in love with him as well.

For a long moment, neither one of them seemed to know what to do, until Paul reached for her hand. With a sigh, Adrienne let him take it, leaning back in her chair as his thumb began to trace her skin.

He smiled, waiting for a response, but Adrienne seemed content to remain quiet. He couldn't read her expression, yet it seemed to hint at everything he was feeling: hope and fear, confusion and acceptance, passion and reserve. But thinking she might need space, he let go of her hand and stood.

"Let me put another log on the fire," he said. "It's getting low."

She nodded, watching him through half-closed eyes as he squatted before the fire, the jeans stretching tight around his thighs.

This couldn't be happening, she told herself. She was forty-five years old, for goodness' sake, not a teenager. She was mature enough to know that something like this couldn't be real. This was the product of the storm, the wine, the fact that they were alone. It was any combination of a thousand things, she told herself, but it wasn't love.

And yet, as she watched Paul add another log and stare quietly into the fireplace, she knew with certainty that it was. The unmistakable look in his eyes, the tremor in his voice as he'd whispered her name . . . she knew his feelings were real. And so, she thought, were hers.

But what did that mean? For him or her? Knowing that he loved her, as wonderful as it was, wasn't the only thing going on here. His look had spoken of desire as well, and that had frightened her, even more than knowing he loved her. Making love, she'd always believed, was more than simply a pleasurable act between two people. It encompassed all that a couple was supposed to share: trust and commitment, hopes and dreams, a promise to make it through whatever the

future may bring. She'd never understood one-night stands or people who
drifted from one bed to the next every
couple of months. It relegated the act to
something almost meaningless, no more
special than a good-night kiss on the
front steps.

Even though they loved each other,
she knew everything would change if she
allowed herself to give in to her feelings.
She would cross a boundary she'd
erected in her mind, and there was no
coming back from something like that.
Making love to Paul would mean that
they would share a bond for the rest of
their lives, and she wasn't sure she was
ready for that.

Nor was she sure she would know
what to do. Jack was not only the only
man she'd ever been with; for eighteen
years, he was the only man she'd *wanted*
to be with. The possibility of sharing
herself with another left her feeling anxious. Making love was a gentle dance
of give-and-take, and the thought she

might disappoint him was almost enough to keep her from letting this go any further.

But she couldn't stop herself. Not anymore. Not with the way he'd looked at her, not with the way she felt about him.

Her throat was dry and her legs felt shaky as she stood from her chair. Paul was still crouching in front of the fire. Moving close, she rested her hands in the soft area between his neck and shoulders. His muscles tightened for an instant, but as she heard him exhale, they relaxed. He turned, looking up at her, and it was then that she felt herself finally give in.

It all felt right to her, he felt right, and as she stood behind him, she knew she would allow herself to go to the place she was meant to be.

Lightning cut the sky outside. Wind and rain were joined as one, pounding against the walls. The room grew hotter as the flames began to leap up again.

Paul stood and faced her. His expression was tender as he reached for her hand. She expected him to kiss her, but he didn't. Instead, he raised her hand and held it against his cheek, closing his eyes, as if wanting to remember her touch against him forever.

Paul kissed the back of her hand before releasing it. Then, opening his eyes and tilting his head, he drew closer until she felt his lips brush against the side of her face in a series of butterfly-light kisses before finally meeting her lips.

She leaned into him then as he wrapped his arms around her; she could feel her breasts pressed against his chest; she could feel the slight stubble on his face when he kissed her the second time.

He ran his hands over her back, her arms, and she parted her lips, feeling the moisture of his tongue. He kissed her neck, her cheek, and as his hand moved around to her belly, his touch was electric. When he moved his hand to her breasts, her breath caught in her throat, and they kissed again and again, the world around them dissolving into something distant and unreal.

It was over now, for both of them, and as they moved even closer, it was as if they were not only embracing each other, but holding all the painful memories at bay.

He buried his hands in her hair, and she leaned her head against his chest, hearing his heart beating as quickly as hers.

Then, when they were finally able to separate, she found herself reaching for his hand.

She took a small step backward and with a gentle pull began leading him to his bedroom upstairs.

Thirteen

In the kitchen, Amanda stared at her mother.

She hadn't spoken since Adrienne had started her story and had gone through two glasses of wine, the second a bit faster than the first. Neither of them was speaking now, and Adrienne could feel the anxious expectation of her daughter as she waited for what would come next.

But Adrienne couldn't tell Amanda about that, nor did she need to. Amanda was a grown woman; she knew what it meant to make love to a man. She was also old enough to know that even though that was a wonderful part of their discovery of each other, it had been just that: a part of it. She loved Paul, and had he not meant so much to her, had the weekend been only physical in nature, there would have been nothing to remember other than a few pleasurable moments, special only because she had been alone so long. What they shared, however, were feelings that had been buried for far too long, feelings that were meant for just the two of them. And only them.

Besides, Amanda was her daughter. Call it old-fashioned, but sharing the details would be inappropriate. Some could talk about such things, but Adrienne never understood how they could. The bedroom, she always thought, was a place of shared secrets.

But even if she'd wanted to tell, she knew she wouldn't be able to find the words. How could she describe the sensation as he began to unbutton her blouse, or the shivers that traveled the length of her body when he traced his finger along her belly? Or how heated

their skin felt as their bodies came together? Or the texture of his mouth
where he kissed her and how she felt
when she pressed her fingers hard into
his skin? Or the sound of his breathing
and hers and how their breaths quickened as they began to move as one?

No, she wouldn't speak of those things.
Instead, she would let her daughter
imagine what had happened, because
Adrienne knew that only her imagination could possibly capture even the
slightest bit of the magic she'd felt in
Paul's arms.

"Mom?" Amanda finally whispered.

"You want to know what happened?"

Amanda swallowed uncomfortably.

"Yes," was all Adrienne would say.

"You mean . . ."

"Yes," she said again.

Amanda took a drink of wine. Steeling
herself, she lowered the glass to the table.
"And? . . ."

Adrienne leaned forward, as if not
wanting anyone to overhear.

"Yes," she whispered, and with that, she glanced off to the side, retreating into the past.

They'd made love that afternoon, and she'd spent the rest of the day in bed. As the storm raged outside—uprooted foliage and wind-whipped trees battering against the house—Paul held her close, his lips pressed against her cheek, each of them recalling the past and together discussing their dreams for the future, both of them marveling over the thoughts and feelings that had led to this moment.

This had been as new for her as it was for Paul. In the last years of her marriage to Jack—maybe most of her marriage, she remembered thinking then—whenever they'd made love, it had been perfunctory, short on passion and quick in time, unmoving with its lack of tenderness. And they seldom talked afterward because Jack usually turned on his side and fell asleep within minutes.

Not only had Paul held her for hours afterward, but his tender embrace let her know that this was just as meaningful to him as the physical intimacy they'd shared. He kissed her hair and face, and every time he caressed a part of her body, he called her beautiful and told her that he adored her in the solemn, sure way she had so quickly come to love.

Though they weren't conscious of it because of the boarded windows, the sky had turned an opaque and angry black. Wind-driven waves battered the dune and washed it away; water lapped at the foundation of the Inn. The antennae on the house was blown away and fell to earth on the opposite end of the island. Sand and rain worked their way through the back door frame as the door vibrated in the energy of the storm. The power went off sometime in the early morning hours. They made love a second time in total darkness, guided by touch, and when they were finished, they finally fell asleep in each other's arms as the eye of the storm passed over Rodanthe.

Fourteen

———◆———

When they woke on Saturday morning, they were famished, but with the power out and the storm slowly winding down, Paul brought the cooler up to the room and they ate in the comfort of bed, alternately laughing and being serious, teasing each other or staying silent, savoring each other and the moment.

By noon, the wind had died down enough for them to venture out and stand on the porch. The sky above them was beginning to clear, but the beach was littered with debris: old tires and washed-out steps from homes that had been set too close to the water and had been caught by the wind-swollen tides. The air was growing warmer; it was still too cold to stay outside without a jacket, but Adrienne removed her gloves so she could feel Paul's hand in her own.

The power came back on with a flicker around two, went out again, and came on for good twenty minutes later. The food in the refrigerator hadn't spoiled, so Adrienne broiled a couple of steaks, and they lingered over a long meal and their third bottle of wine. Afterward they took a bath together. Paul sat behind her, and as she rested her head on his chest, he ran the washcloth over her stomach and breasts. Adrienne closed her eyes, sinking into his arms, feeling the warm water wash over her skin.

That night, they went into town. Rodanthe was coming back to life after the storm, and they spent part of the evening in a dingy bar, listening to music from the jukebox and dancing to a few of

the songs. The bar was crowded with lo-
cals who wanted to share their stories of
the storm, and Paul and Adrienne were
the only ones who braved the floor. He
pulled her close and they rotated slowly
in circles, her body against his, oblivious
to the chatter and stares from the other
patrons.

On Sunday, Paul took down the hurricane guards and stored them, then put
the rockers back in place on the porch.
The sky had cleared for the first time
since the storm, and they walked the
beach, just as they'd done on their first
night together, noticing how much had
changed since then. The ocean had
carved long, violent grooves where it
had washed away parts of the beach, and
a number of trees had toppled over. Less
than half a mile away, Paul and Adrienne
found themselves staring at a house, half
on the pilings, half on the sand, that had
been victim to the storm surge. Most of
the walls had buckled, the windows were

smashed, and part of the roof had blown away. A dishwasher lay on its side near a pile of broken slats that once looked to be the porch. Near the road, a group of people had gathered, taking pictures for insurance purposes, and for the first time they realized how bad the storm had really been.

When they started back, the tide was rolling in. They were walking slowly, their shoulders touching slightly, when they came across the conch. Its ribboned exterior was half-buried in the sand and surrounded by thousands of tiny fragments of broken shells. When Paul handed it to her, she raised it to her ear, and it was then that he teased her about her claim to hear the ocean. He put his arms around her then, telling her that she was as perfect as the shell they'd just found. Although Adrienne knew she would keep it forever, she didn't have any idea of how much it would eventually come to mean to her.

All she knew was that she was standing in the arms of a man she loved, wishing that he would be able to hold her this way forever.

———◆———

On Monday morning, Paul slipped out of bed before she was awake, and though he'd claimed ignorance in the kitchen, he surprised her by bringing breakfast to her on a tray in bed, rousing her with the aroma of fresh coffee. He sat with her as she ate, laughing as she leaned against the pillows, trying and failing to keep the sheet high enough to cover her breasts. The French toast was delicious, the bacon was crispy without being burned, and he'd added just the right amount of grated cheddar cheese to the scrambled eggs.

Though her children had occasionally made her breakfast in bed on Mother's Day, it was the first time a man had ever done that for her. Jack had never been the type to think of such things.

When she was finished, Paul went for a short jog as Adrienne showered and dressed. After his run, Paul threw his dirty clothes into the washer and showered as well. By the time he had joined her in the kitchen again, Adrienne was on the phone to Jean. She'd called to find out how everything had gone. As Adrienne filled her in, Paul slipped his arms around her, nuzzling the back of her neck.

While on the phone, Adrienne heard the unmistakable sound of the front door of the Inn squeaking open and the entrance of work boots clicking against the wooden floor. She said as much to Jean before hanging up, then left the kitchen to see who had entered. She was gone for less than a minute before she returned, and when she did, she looked at Paul as if at a loss for words. She drew a long breath.

"He's here to talk to you," she said.

"Who?"

"Robert Torrelson."

———•◦•———

Robert Torrelson waited in the sitting room and was seated on the couch with his head bowed when Paul went to join him. He looked up without smiling, his face unreadable. Before he'd come, Paul wasn't sure he could have picked Robert Torrelson from a crowd, but up close, he realized he recognized the man sitting before him. Other than his hair, which had grown whiter in the past year, he looked the same as he had in the waiting room of the hospital. His eyes were as hard as Paul had imagined they would be.

Robert said nothing right away. Instead, he stared as Paul angled the rocker so they could face each other.

"You came," Robert Torrelson finally said. His voice was strong and raspy, southern made, as if cured by years of smoking unfiltered Camel cigarettes.

"Yes."

"I didn't think you would."

"For a while, I wasn't sure whether I would, either."

Robert snorted as if he'd expected that. "My son said he talked to you."

"He did."

Robert smiled bitterly, knowing what had been said. "He said you didn't try to explain yourself."

"No," Paul answered, "I didn't."

"But you still don't think you did anything wrong, do you?"

Paul glanced away, thinking about what Adrienne had said. No, he thought, he'd never change their minds. He straightened up.

"In your letter, you said you wanted to talk to me and that it was important. And now I'm here. What can I do for you, Mr. Torrelson?"

Robert reached into the front pocket of his shirt and pulled out a pack of cigarettes and a book of matches. He lit one, moved an ashtray closer, and leaned back on the couch.

"What went wrong?" he asked.

"Nothing," Paul said. "The operation went as well as I'd hoped."

"Then why did she die?"

"I wish I knew, but I don't."

"Is that what your lawyers told you to say?"

"No," Paul responded evenly, "it's the truth. I thought that's what you'd want to hear. If I could give you an answer, I would."

Robert brought the cigarette to his mouth and inhaled. When he exhaled, Paul could hear a slight wheeze, like air escaping from an old accordion.

"Did you know she had the tumor when we first met?"

"No," Paul said. "I didn't."

Robert took another long drag on his cigarette. When he spoke again, his voice was softer, shaded with memory.

"It wasn't as big then, of course. It was

more like a half a walnut, and the color wasn't so bad, either. But you could still see it plain as day, like something was wedged under her skin. And it always bothered her, even when she was little. I'm a few years older than she was, and I remember that she always used to look at her shoes when she walked to school, and it didn't take much to know why."

Robert paused, collecting his thoughts, and Paul knew enough to stay silent.

"Like a lot of folks back then, she didn't finish her schooling because she had to work to help the family, and that's when I first got to know her. She worked at the pier where we'd unload our catch, and she ran the scales. I probably tried to talk to her for a year before she said a single word to me, but I liked her anyway. She was honest and she worked hard, and even though she used her hair to keep her face hidden, every now and then I got the chance to see what was underneath, and I'd find myself looking into the prettiest eyes I'd ever seen. They were dark brown, and soft, you know? Like she'd never hurt a soul in her life because it just wasn't in her. And I kept trying to talk to her and she just kept ignoring me until I guess she finally figured that I wasn't going to let up. She let me take her out, but she barely looked at me all night long. Just kept staring at those shoes."

Robert brought his hands together.

"But I asked her out again anyway. It was better the second time, and I realized that she was funny when she wanted to be. The more I got to know her, the more I liked her, and then after a while, I started to think that maybe I was in love with her. I didn't care about that thing on her face. Didn't care about it back then, and I didn't care about it last year, either. But she did. She always did."

He paused.

"We had seven kids over the next twenty years, and it seemed like every time she was nursing one of 'em, that thing grew more. I don't know if it was true or not, but she used to tell me the same thing. But all my kids, even John— the one you met—thought she was the best mom around. And she was. She was tough when she needed to be and the sweetest lady you ever met the rest of the time. And I loved her for that, and we were happy. Life here ain't easy most of the time, but she made it easy for me. And I was proud of her, and I was proud to be seen with her, and I made sure that everyone around here knew that. I thought that would be enough, but I guess it wasn't."

Paul remained motionless as Robert went on.

"She saw this show on television one night about a lady with one of those tumor things, and it had those before and after pictures. I think she just got it in her head that she could get rid of it once and for all. And that was when she started talking about getting an operation. It was expensive and we didn't have insurance, but she kept asking if there was some way we could do it."

Robert met Paul's eyes.

"There was nothing I could say to her to change her mind. I'd tell her I didn't care about it, but she wouldn't listen. Sometimes, I'd find her in the bathroom touching her face, or I'd hear her crying, and I knew she wanted it more than anything. She'd lived with this thing her whole life, and she was tired of it. Tired of the way strangers used to avoid looking at her, or how kids would stare too long. So I finally gave in. I took all our savings, went to the bank and got a loan against my boat, and we went to see you. She was so excited that morning. I don't think I'd ever seen her so happy about anything in her life, and just seeing her that way let me know I was doing the right thing. I told her that I'd be waiting for her and would come to see her just as soon as she woke up, and do you know what she said to me? What her last words to me were?"

Robert looked at Paul, making sure he had his attention.

"She said, 'All my life, I've wanted to be pretty for you.' And all I could think when she said it was that she always had been."

Paul bowed his head, and though he tried to swallow, there was a catch in his throat.

"But you didn't know any of those things about her. To you, she was just the lady who came in for an operation, or the lady who died, or the lady with the thing on her face, or the lady whose family was suing you. It wasn't right for you not to know her story. She deserved more than that. She earned more than that by living the life she did."

Robert Torrelson tapped the last of his ashes into the ashtray, then put out the cigarette.

"You were the last person she ever talked to, the last person she saw in her life. She was the best lady in the world, and you didn't even know who you were seeing." He paused, letting that sink in. "But now you do."

With that, he stood from the couch, and a moment later he was gone.

———

After hearing what Robert Torrelson had said, Adrienne touched Paul's face, dabbing away his tears.

"You okay?"

"I don't know," he said. "I'm kind of numb right now."

"That's not surprising. It was a lot to absorb."

"Yes," Paul said, "it was."

"Are you glad you came? And that he told you those things?"

"Yes and no. It was important to him that I know who she was, so I'm glad for that. But it makes me sad, too. They loved each other so much, and now she's gone."

"Yes."

"It doesn't seem fair."

She offered a wistful smile. "It isn't. The greater the love, the greater the tragedy when it's over. Those two elements always go together."

"Even for you and me?"

"For everyone," she said. "The best we can hope for in life is that it doesn't happen for a long, long time."

He pulled her onto his lap. He kissed her lips, then put his arms around her, holding her close, letting her hold him, and for a long time, they stayed in that position.

But as they were making love later that evening, Adrienne's words came back to her. It was their last night together in Rodanthe, their last night together for at least a year. And as much as she tried to fight them, she couldn't stop the tears as they slipped silently down her cheeks.

Fifteen

⟶•⟵

Adrienne wasn't in the bed when Paul woke on Tuesday morning. He'd seen her crying during the night but had said nothing, knowing that speaking would bring him to tears as well. But the denial left him ragged and unable to sleep for hours. Instead, he lay awake as she fell asleep in his arms, nuzzling against her, not wanting to let go, as if trying to make up for the year they wouldn't be together.

She'd folded his clothes for him, the ones that had been in the dryer, and Paul pulled out what he needed for the day before packing the rest in his duffel bags.

After he showered and dressed, he sat on the side of the bed, pen in hand, scribbling his thoughts on paper. Leaving the note in his room, he brought his things downstairs and left them near the front door. Adrienne was in the kitchen, standing over the stove and stirring a pan of scrambled eggs, a cup of coffee on the counter beside her. When she turned, he could see that her eyes were rimmed in red.

"Hi," he ventured.

"Hi," she said, turning away. She began stirring the eggs more quickly, keeping her eyes at the pan. "I figured you might want some breakfast before you go."

"Thank you," he said.

"I brought a thermos from home when I came, and if you want some coffee for the trip, you can take it with you."

"Thank you, but that's okay. I'll be fine."

She kept stirring the eggs. "If you want a couple of sandwiches, I can throw those together, too."

Paul moved toward her. "You don't

have to do that. I can get something later. And to be honest, I doubt if I'll be hungry anyway."

She didn't seem to be listening, and he put his hand on her back. He heard her exhale shakily, as if trying to keep from crying.

Hey . . ."

"I'm okay," she whispered.

"You sure?"

She nodded and sniffed as she removed the pan from the burner. Dabbing at her eyes, she still refused to look at him. Seeing her this way reminded him of their first encounter on the porch, and he felt his throat constrict. He couldn't believe that less than a week had passed since then.

"Adrienne . . . don't . . ."

She looked up at him then.

"Don't what? Be sad? You're going to Ecuador and I have to go back to Rocky Mount. Can I help it if I don't want this to end just yet?"

"I don't either."

"And that's why I'm sad. Because I know that, too." She hesitated, trying to stay in control of her feelings. "You know, when I got up this morning, I told myself I wasn't going to cry again. I told myself that I'd be strong and happy, so that you would remember me that way. But when I heard the shower come on, it just hit me that when I wake up to-morrow, you're not going to be here, and I couldn't help it. But I'll be okay. I really will. I'm tough."

She said it as though she were trying to convince herself. Paul reached for her hand.

"Adrienne . . . last night, after you went to sleep, I got to thinking that maybe I could stay a little while longer. Another month or two isn't going to make much difference, and that way we could be together—"

She shook her head, cutting him off.

"No," she said. "You can't do that to Mark. Not after all that you two have been through. And you need this, Paul.

It's been eating you up; if you don't go now, part of me wonders if you ever will. Spending more time with me isn't going to make it any easier to say good-bye when the time comes, and I couldn't live with myself knowing that I was the one who kept you and your son apart. Even if we planned for your leaving the next time, I'd still cry then, too."

She flashed a brave smile before going on. "You can't stay. We both knew you were leaving before the *we* part of us even began. Even though it's hard, both of us also know it's the right thing to do—that's the way it is when you're a parent. Sometimes there are sacrifices you have to make, and this is one of them."

He nodded, his lips pressed together. He knew she was right but wished desperately that she wasn't.

"Will you promise that you'll wait for me?" he asked finally, his voice ragged.

"Of course. If I thought you were leaving forever, I'd be crying so hard, we'd have to eat breakfast in a rowboat."

Despite everything he laughed, and Adrienne leaned into him. She kissed him before letting him hold her. He could feel the warmth of her body, smell the faintest trace of perfume. She felt so good in his arms. So perfect.

"I don't know how or why it happened, but I think I was meant to come here," he said. "To meet you. For so many years, I've been missing something in my life, but I didn't know what it was. And now I do."

She closed her eyes. "Me too," she whispered.

He kissed her hair, then rested his cheek against her.

"Will you miss me?"

Adrienne forced herself to smile. "Every single minute."

———⋅◆⋅———

They had breakfast together. Adrienne wasn't hungry, but she forced herself to eat, forced herself to smile now and then.

Paul picked at his food, taking longer than usual to clean his plate, and when they were finished, they brought the dishes to the sink.

It was almost nine o'clock, and Paul led her past the front desk toward the door. He lifted one duffel bag at a time to sling over his shoulders; Adrienne held the leather pouch with his tickets and passport, which she handed to him.

"I guess this is it," he said.

Adrienne pressed her lips together. Like hers, Paul's eyes were red around the edges, and he kept them downcast, as if trying to hide them.

"You know how to reach me at the clinic. I don't know how good the mail service is, but letters should reach me. Mark's always gotten everything Martha has sent him."

"Thanks."

He shook the pouch. "I have your address, too, in here. I'll write to you when I get there. And call, too, when I get the chance."

"Okay."

He reached out to touch her cheek, and she leaned into his hand. They both knew there wasn't anything more to say.

She followed him out the door and down the steps, watching as he loaded the duffel bags into the backseat. After closing the door, he stared at her a long time, unwilling to break the connection, wishing again that he didn't have to go. Finally he moved toward her, kissed her on both cheeks and on her lips. He took her in his arms.

Adrienne squeezed her eyes shut. He wasn't leaving forever, she told herself. They were meant for each other; they would have all the time in the world when he got back. They would grow old together. She'd lived this long without him already—what was one more year, right?

But it wasn't that easy. She knew that if her children were older, she would join him in Ecuador. If his son didn't need him, he could stay here, with her.

Their lives were diverging because of responsibilities to others, and it suddenly seemed cruelly unfair to Adrienne. How could their chance at happiness come down to this?

Paul took a deep breath and finally moved away. He glanced to the side for a moment, then back at her, dabbing at his eyes.

She followed him around to the driver's side and watched as he got in. With a weak smile, he put the key in the ignition and turned it, revving the engine to life. She stepped back from the open door and he closed it, then rolled down the window.

"One year," he said, "and I'll be back. You have my word on that."

"One year," she whispered in response.

He gave her a sad smile, then put the car in reverse, and with that, the car began backing out. She turned to watch him, aching inside as he stared back at her.

The car turned as it reached the highway, and he pressed his hand to the glass one last time. Adrienne raised her hand, watching the car roll forward, away from Rodanthe, away from her.

She stood in the drive as the car grew smaller in the distance and the noise of the engine faded away. Then, a moment later, he was gone, as if he'd never been there at all.

The morning was crisp, blue skies with puffs of white. A flock of terns flew overhead. Purple and yellow pansies had opened their petals to the sun. Adrienne turned and made her way toward the door.

Inside, it looked the same as the day she'd arrived. Nothing was out of place. He'd cleaned the fireplace yesterday and stacked new cords of wood beside it; the rockers had been put back into their original position. The front desk looked orderly, with every key back in its place.

But the smell remained. The smell of their breakfast together, the smell of after have, the smell of him, lingering on her hands and on her face and on her clothes.

It was too much for Adrienne, and the noises of the Inn at Rodanthe were no longer what they had once been. No longer were there echoes of quiet conversations, or the sound of water rushing through the pipes, or the rhythm of footfalls as he moved about in his room. Gone was the roar of waves and the persistent drumming of the storm, the crackling of the fire. Instead, the Inn was filled with the sounds of a woman who wanted only to be comforted by the man she loved, a woman who could do nothing else but cry.

Sixteen

Rocky Mount, 2002

Adrienne had finished her story, and her throat was dry. Despite the breezy effects of a single glass of wine, she could feel the ache in her back from sitting in one position too long. She shifted in her chair, felt a tinge of pain, and recognized it as the beginnings of arthritis. When she'd mentioned it to her physician, he'd made her sit on the table in a room that smelled of ammonia. He'd raised her arms and asked her to bend her knees, then given her a prescription that she'd never bothered to fill. It wasn't that serious yet, she told herself; besides, she had a theory that once she started taking pills for one ailment, more pills would soon follow for everything else that doomed people of her age. Soon, they'd be coming in the color of rainbows, some taken in the morning, others at night, some with food and some without, and she'd need to tape up a chart on the inside of her medicine cabinet to keep them straight. It was more bother than it was worth.

Amanda was sitting with her head bowed. Adrienne watched her, knowing the questions would come. They were inevitable, but she hoped they wouldn't come immediately. She needed time to collect her thoughts, so she could finish what she'd started.

She was glad Amanda had agreed to meet her here, at the house. She'd lived here for over thirty years, and it was home to her, even more than the place she'd lived as a child. Granted, some of the doors hung crookedly, the carpet was worn paper thin in the hallway, and the colors of the bathroom tiles had been out of style for years, but there was something reassuring about knowing that she could find camping gear in the far left corner of the attic or that the heat pump would trip the fuse the first time it was used in the winter. This place had habits; so did she, and over the years, she supposed they'd meshed in such a way as to make her life more predictable and oddly comforting.

It was the same in the kitchen. Both Matt and Dan had been offering to have it remodeled for the last couple of years, and for her birthday they'd arranged to have a contractor come through to look the place over. He'd tapped on doors, jabbed his screwdriver in the corners of the cracking counters, turned the switches on and off, and whistled under his breath when he saw the ancient range she still used to cook. In the end, he'd recommended she replace just about everything, then dropped off an estimate and a list of references. Though Adrienne knew her sons had meant well, she told them that they'd be better off saving the money for something they needed for their own families.

Besides, she liked the old kitchen as it was. Updating it would change its character, and she liked the memories forged here. It was here, after all, that they'd spent most of their time together as a family, both before and after Jack had moved out. The kids had done their homework at the table where she now sat; for years, the only phone in the house hung on the wall, and she could still remember those times when she'd seen the cord wedged between the back door and the frame as one of the kids tried his or her best for a bit of privacy by standing on the porch. On the shelf supports in the pantry were the pencil markings that showed how fast and tall the children had grown over the years, and she couldn't imagine wanting to get rid of that for something new and improved, no matter how fancy it was. Unlike the living room, where the television continually blared, or the bedrooms where everyone retreated to be alone, this was the one place everyone had come to talk and listen, to learn and to teach, to laugh and to cry. This was the place where their home was what it was supposed to be; this was the place where Adrienne had always felt most content.

And this was the place where Amanda would learn who her mother really was.

———◆———

Adrienne drank the last of her wine and pushed the glass aside. The rain had stopped now, but the drops remaining on the window seemed to bend the light in such a way as to make the world outside into something different, a place she couldn't quite recognize. This didn't surprise her; as she'd grown older, she'd found that as her thoughts drifted to the past, everything around her always seemed to change. Tonight, as she told her story, she felt as if the intervening years had been reversed, and though it was a ridiculous notion, she wondered if her daughter had noticed a newfound youthfulness about her.

No, she decided, she almost certainly hadn't, but that was a product of Amanda's age. Amanda could no more conceive of being sixty than she could of being a man, and Adrienne sometimes wondered when Amanda would realize that for the most part, people weren't all that different. Young and old, male or female, pretty much everyone she knew wanted the same things: They wanted to feel peace in their hearts, they wanted a life without turmoil, they wanted to be happy. The difference, Adrienne thought, was that most young people seemed to think that those things lay somewhere in the future, while most older people believed that they lay in the past.

It was true for her as well, at least partly, but as wonderful as the past had been, she refused to allow herself to remain lost in it the way many of her friends had. The past wasn't merely a garden of roses and sunshine; the past held its share of heartbreak as well. She had felt that way about Jack's effects on her life when she'd first arrived at the Inn, and she felt that way now about Paul Flanner.

Tonight, she would cry, but as she had promised herself every day since he'd left Rodanthe, she would go on. She was a survivor, as her father had told her many times, and though there was a certain satisfaction to that knowledge, it didn't erase the pain or regrets.

Nowadays, she tried to focus on those things that brought her joy. She loved to watch the grandchildren as they discovered the world, she loved to visit with friends and find out what was happening in their lives, she had even come to enjoy the days she spent working in the library.

The work wasn't hard—she now worked in the special reference section,

where books couldn't be checked out—
and because hours might pass before she
was needed for something, it offered her
the opportunity to watch people who
pushed through the glassed entryway of
the building. She'd developed a fondness
for that over the years. As people sat at
the tables or in the chairs in the quiet
rooms, she found it impossible not to try
to imagine their lives. She would try to
figure out if a person was married or
what she did for a living, where in town
she lived, or what books might interest
her, and occasionally, she would have the
chance to find out whether she'd been
right. The person might come to her for
help in finding a particular book, and
she'd strike up a friendly conversation.
More often than not, she'd end up being
fairly close in her guesses and would
wonder how she'd known.

Every now and then, someone would
come in who was interested in her. Years
ago, those men had usually been older
than she was; now they tended to be

younger, but either way, the process was the same. Whoever he was, he would start spending time in special reference, would ask a lot of questions, first about books, then about general topics, and finally about her. She didn't mind answering them, and though she never led them on, most of them eventually asked her out. She was always a bit flattered when that happened, but at her core she knew that no matter how wonderful this suitor might be, no matter how much she enjoyed his company, she wouldn't be able to open her heart to him in the way she once had done.

Her time in Rodanthe had changed her in other ways as well. Being with Paul had healed her feelings of loss and betrayal over the divorce and replaced them with something stronger and more graceful. Knowing that she was worthy of being loved made it easier to hold her head high, and as her confidence grew, she was able to speak to Jack without hidden meanings or insinuations, without the blame and regret that she'd been unable to hide in her tone in the past. It happened gradually; he'd call to talk to the kids, and they'd visit for a few minutes before she handed off the phone. Later, she'd begun asking about Linda or his job, or she'd fill him in on what she'd been doing recently. Little by little, Jack seemed to realize that she was no longer the person she used to be. Those visits became more friendly with the passing months and years, and sometimes they called each other just to chat. When his marriage to Linda started to unravel, they'd spent hours on the phone, sometimes until late in the night. When Jack and Linda divorced, Adrienne had been there to help him through his grief, and she'd even allowed him to stay in the guest bedroom when he came to see the kids. Ironically, Linda had left him for another man, and Adrienne could remember sitting with Jack in the living room as he swirled a glass of Scotch. It was past midnight, and he'd been rambling for a few hours about what he was going through, when he finally seemed to realize who it was that was listening to him.

"Did it hurt this bad for you?" he asked.

"Yes," Adrienne said.

"How long did it take to get over it?"

"Three years," she said, "but I was lucky."

Jack nodded. Pressing his lips together, he stared into his drink.

"I'm sorry," he said. "The dumbest thing I ever did was to walk out that door."

Adrienne smiled and patted his knee. "I know. But thank you anyway."

It was about a year after that when Jack called to ask her to dinner. And as she had with all the others, Adrienne politely said no.

Adrienne rose and went to the counter to retrieve the box she'd carried from her bedroom earlier, then came back to the table. By then, Amanda was watching her with almost wary fascination. Adrienne smiled as she reached for her daughter's hand.

As she did, Adrienne could see that sometime during the past couple of hours, Amanda had realized that she didn't know as much about her mother as she thought she did. It was, Adrienne thought, a role reversal of sorts. Amanda had the same look in her eyes that Adrienne sometimes had in the past, when the kids would get together over the holidays and joke about some of the things they'd done when they were younger. It was only a couple of years ago that she'd learned that Matt used to sneak out of his room to go out with friends late at night, or that Amanda had both started and quit smoking as a junior, or that Dan had been the one who'd started the small fire in the garage that had been blamed on a faulty electrical outlet. She'd laughed along with them, feeling naive at the same time, and she wondered if that was the way Amanda was feeling now.

On the wall, the clock was ticking, the sound regular and even. The heat pump clicked on with a thump. In time, Amanda sighed.

"That was quite a story," she said.

As she spoke, Amanda fingered her wineglass with her free hand, rotating it in circles. The wine caught the light, making it shimmer.

"Do Matt and Dan know? I mean, have you told them about it?"

"No."

"Why not?"

"I'm not sure they need to know." Adrienne smiled. "And besides, I don't know if they would understand, no matter what I told them. They're men, for one thing, and a little on the protective side—I don't want them to think that Paul was simply preying on a lonely woman. Men are like that sometimes—if they meet someone and fall in love, it's real, no matter how fast it happened. But if someone falls for a woman they happen to care about, all they do is question the man's intentions. To be honest, I don't know if I'll ever tell them."

Amanda nodded before asking, "Why me, then?"

"Because I thought you needed to hear it."

Absently, Amanda began to twirl a strand of hair. Adrienne wondered if that habit was genetic or learned by watching her mother.

"Mom?"

"Yes?"

"Why didn't you tell us about him? I mean, you never mentioned anything about it."

"I couldn't."

"Why not?"

Adrienne leaned back in her chair and took a deep breath. "In the beginning, I guess I was afraid it wasn't real. I know we loved each other, but distance can do strange things to people, and before I was willing to tell you about it, I wanted to be certain that it would last. Then later, when I started getting letters from him and knew it would . . . I don't know . . . it just seemed such a long time until you could meet him that I didn't see the point in it. . . ."

She trailed off before choosing her next words carefully.

"You also have to realize that you're not the same person now that you were then. You were seventeen, Dan was only fifteen, and I didn't know if any of you were ready to hear something like this. I mean, how would you have felt if you'd come back from your father's and I told you that I was in love with someone I'd just met?"

"We could've handled it."

Adrienne was skeptical about that, but she didn't argue with Amanda. Instead, she shrugged. "Who knows. Maybe you're right. Maybe you could have accepted something like this, but at the time, I didn't want to take the chance. And if I had to do it all over, I'd probably do the same thing again."

Amanda shifted in her chair. After a moment, she looked her mother in the eye. "Are you sure he loved you?" she asked.

"Yes," she said.

Amanda's eyes looked almost blue green in the fading light. She smiled gently, as if trying to make an obvious point without hurting her mother.

Adrienne knew what Amanda would ask next. It was, she thought, the only logical question left.

Amanda leaned forward, her face filled with concern. "Then where is he?"

＊＊＊

In the fourteen years since she'd last seen Paul Flanner, Adrienne had traveled to Rodanthe five times. Her first trip had been during June of the same year, and though the sand seemed whiter and the ocean melted into the sky at the horizon, she made the remainder of her trips during the winter months, when the world was gray and cold, knowing that it was a more potent reminder of the past.

On the morning that Paul left, Adrienne wandered the house, unable to stay in one place. Movement seemed to be the only way she could stay ahead of her feelings. Late in the afternoon, as dusk was beginning to dress the sky in faded shades of red and orange, she went outside and looked into those colors, trying to find the plane that Paul was on. The odds of seeing it were infinitesimal, but she stayed out anyway, growing chilled as the evening deepened. Between the clouds, she saw an occasional jet trail, but logic told her they were from planes stationed at the naval base in Norfolk. By the time she went in, her hands were numb, and at the sink she ran warm tap water over them, feeling the sting. Though she understood that he was gone, she set two place settings at the dinner table just the same.

Part of her had hoped he would come back. As she ate her dinner, she imagined him coming through the front door and dropping his bags, explaining that he couldn't leave without another night together. They would leave tomorrow or the next day, he would say, and they would follow the highway north, until she made the turn for home.

But he didn't. The front door never swung open, the phone never rang. As much as Adrienne longed for him to stay, she knew she'd been right when she'd urged him on his way. Another day wouldn't make it easier to leave; another night together would only mean they'd have to say good-bye again, and that had been hard enough the first time. She couldn't imagine having to say those words a second time, nor could she imagine having to relive another day like the one she had just spent.

The following morning, she began cleaning the Inn, moving steadily, focusing on the routine. She washed the dishes and made sure everything was dried and put away. She vacuumed the area rugs, she swept the sand from the kitchen and entranceway, she dusted the balustrade and lamps in the sitting room, then she worked on Jean's room until she was satisfied that it looked the same as when she'd arrived.

Then, after carrying her suitcase upstairs, she unlocked the door to the blue room.

She hadn't been in there since the morning Paul had left. The afternoon sunlight cast prisms on the walls. He'd fixed the bed before he'd gone downstairs but seemed to have realized that he didn't need to make it neat. There were slight bulges under the comforter where the blanket had wrinkled, and the sheet poked out in a few places, nearly grazing the floor. In the bathroom, a towel hung over the curtain rod, and two more had been lumped together near the sink.

She stood without moving, taking it all in, before finally exhaling and putting down her suitcase. As she did, she saw the note that Paul had written her, propped on the bureau. She reached for it and slowly sat on the edge of the bed. In the quiet of the room where they'd loved each other, she read what he had penned the morning before.

When she was finished, Adrienne lowered the note and sat without moving, thinking of him as he'd written it. Then, after folding it carefully, she put it it into her suitcase along with the conch. When Jean arrived a few hours later, Adrienne was leaning against the railing on the back porch, looking toward the sky again.

Jean was her normal, exuberant self, happy to see Adrienne, happy to be back home, and talking incessantly about the wedding and the old hotel in Savannah where she had stayed. Adrienne let Jean go on with her stories without interruption, and after dinner, she told Jean that she wanted to take a walk on the beach. Thankfully, Jean passed on the invitation to go with her.

When she got back, Jean was unpacking in her room, and Adrienne made herself a cup of hot tea and went to sit near the fireplace. As she was rocking, she heard Jean enter the kitchen.

"Where are you?" Jean called out.

"In here," Adrienne answered.

Jean rounded the corner a moment later. "Did I hear the teakettle whistle?"

"I just made a cup."

"Since when do you drink tea?"

Adrienne gave a short laugh but didn't answer.

Jean settled in the rocker beside her. Outside, the moon was rising, hard and brilliant, making the sand glow with the color of antique pots and pans.

"You've been kind of quiet tonight," Jean said.

"Sorry." Adrienne shrugged. "I'm just a little tired. I guess I'm just ready to go home."

"I'm sure. I was counting the miles as soon as I left Savannah, but at least there wasn't much traffic. Off-season, you know."

Adrienne nodded.

Jean leaned back in her chair. "Did it go okay with Paul Flanner? I hope the storm didn't ruin his stay."

Hearing his name made Adrienne's throat catch, but she tried to appear calm. "I don't think the storm bothered him at all," she said.

"Tell me about him. From his voice, I got the impression that he was kind of stuffy."

"No, not all. He was . . . nice."

"Was it strange being alone with him?"

"No. Not once I got used to it."

Jean waited to see if Adrienne would add anything else, but she didn't.

"Well . . . good," Jean continued. "And you didn't have any trouble boarding up the house?"

"No."

"I'm glad. I appreciate your doing that for me. I know you were hoping for a quiet weekend, but I guess fate wasn't on your side, huh?"

"I suppose not."

Perhaps it was the way she said it that drew Jean's glance, a curious expression on her face. Suddenly needing space, Adrienne finished her tea.

"I hate to do this to you, Jean," she said, trying her best to make her voice sound natural, "but I think I'll call it a night. I'm tired, and I've got a long drive tomorrow. I'm glad you had a good time at the wedding."

Jean's eyebrows rose slightly at her friend's abrupt ending to the evening.

"Oh . . . well, thank you," she said. "Good night."

"Good night."

Adrienne could feel Jean's uncertain

gaze on her, even as she made her way up the stairs. After unlocking the door to the blue room, she slipped out of her clothes and crawled into the bed, naked and alone.

She could smell Paul on the pillow and on the sheets, and she absently traced her breast as she buried herself in the smell, fighting sleep until she could do so no longer. When she rose the following morning, she started a pot of coffee and took another walk on the beach.

She passed two other couples in the half hour she spent outside. A front had pushed warmer air over the island, and she knew the day would lure even more people to the water's edge.

Paul would have arrived at the clinic by now, and she wondered what it was like. She had an image in her mind, something she might have seen on one of the nature channels—a series of hastily assembled buildings surrounded by an encroaching jungle, ruts in a curving dirt road out front, exotic birds chirping in the background—but she doubted that she was right. She wondered if he had talked to Mark yet and how the meeting had gone, and whether Paul, like she, was still reliving the weekend in his mind.

The kitchen was empty when she got back. She could see the sugar bowl open by the coffeemaker with an empty cup beside it. Upstairs, she could hear the faint sound of someone humming.

Adrienne followed the sound, and when she reached the second floor, she could see the door to the blue room cracked open. Adrienne drew nearer, pushing the door open farther, and saw Jean bending over, tucking in the final corner of a fresh sheet. The old linens, the linen that had once wrapped her and Paul together, had been bundled and tossed on the floor.

Adrienne stared at the sheets, knowing it was ridiculous to be upset but suddenly realizing it would be at least a year until she smelled Paul Flanner again. She inhaled raggedly, trying to stifle a cry.

Jean turned in surprise at the sound, her eyes wide.

"Adrienne?" she asked. "Are you okay?"

But Adrienne couldn't answer. All she could do was bring her hands to her face, aware that from this point on, she would be marking the days on the calendar until Paul returned.

"Paul," Adrienne answered her daughter, "is in Ecuador." Her voice, she noted, was surprisingly steady.

"Ecuador," Amanda repeated. Her fingers tapped the table as she stared at her mother. "Why didn't he come back?"

"He couldn't."

"Why not?"

Instead of answering, Adrienne lifted

the lid of the stationery box. From in-side, she pulled out a piece of paper that looked to Amanda as if it had been torn from a student's notebook. Folded over, it had yellowed with age. Amanda saw her mother's name written across the front.

"Before I tell you," Adrienne went on, "I want to answer your other question."

"What other question?"

Adrienne smiled. "You asked whether I was sure that Paul loved me." She slid the piece of paper across the table to her daughter. "This is the note he wrote to me on the day that he left."

Amanda hesitated before taking it, then slowly unfolded the paper. With her mother sitting across from her, she began to read.

Dear Adrienne,
You weren't beside me when I woke this morning, and though I know why you left, I wish you hadn't. I know that's

selfish of me, but I suppose that's one of the traits that's stayed with me, the one constant in my life.

If you're reading this, it means I've left. When I'm finished writing, I'm going to go downstairs and ask to stay with you longer, but I'm under no illusions as to what you're going to say to me.

This isn't a good-bye, and I don't want you to think for a moment that it's the reason for this letter. Rather, I'm going to look at the year ahead as a chance to get to know you even better than I do. I've heard of people falling in love through letters, and though we're already there, it doesn't mean our love can't grow deeper, does it? I'd like to think it's possible, and if you want to know the truth, that conviction is the only thing I expect to help me make it through the next year without you.

If I close my eyes, I can see you walking along the beach on our first night together. With lightning flickering on your face, you were absolutely beautiful, and I think that's part of the reason I was able to open up to you in a way I never had with anyone else. But it wasn't just your beauty that moved me. It was everything you are—your courage and your passion, the commonsense wisdom with which you view the world. I think I sensed these things about you the first time we had coffee, and if anything, the more I got to know you, the more I realized how much I'd missed these qualities in my own life. You are a rare find, Adrienne, and I'm a lucky man for having had the chance to come to know you.

I hope that you're doing okay. As I write this letter, I know that I'm not. Saying good-bye to you today is the hardest thing I'll ever have to do, and when I get back, I can honestly swear that I'll never do it again. I love you now for what we've already shared, and I love you now in anticipation of all that's to come. You are the best thing that's ever happened to me. I miss you already, but I'm sure in my heart that you'll be with me always.

*In the few days I spent with you, you be-
came my dream.*

Paul

———◆———

The year following Paul's departure
was unlike any year in Adrienne's life.
On the surface, things went on as usual.
She was active in her children's life, she
visited with her father once a day, she
worked at the library as she always had.
But she carried with her a new zest, fu-
eled by the secret she kept inside, and the
change in her attitude wasn't lost on people around her. She smiled more, they
sometimes commented, and even her
children occasionally noticed that she
took walks after dinner or spent an hour
now and then lingering in the tub,
ignoring the mayhem around her.

She thought of Paul always in those
moments, but his image was most real
whenever she saw the mail truck coming

up the road, stopping and starting with each delivery on the route.

The mail usually arrived between ten and eleven in the morning, and Adrienne would stand by the window, watching as the truck paused in front of her house. Once it was gone, she would walk to the box and sort through the bundle, looking for the telltale signs of his letters: the beige airmail envelopes he favored, postage stamps that depicted a world she knew nothing about, his name scrawled in the upper-left-hand corner.

When his first letter arrived, she read it on the back porch. As soon as she was finished, she started from the beginning and read it a second time more slowly, pausing and lingering over his words. She did the same with each subsequent letter, and as they began to arrive regularly, she realized that the message in Paul's note had been true. Though it wasn't as gratifying as seeing him or feeling his arms around her, the passion in his words somehow made the distance between them seem that much less.

She loved to imagine how he looked as he wrote the letters. She pictured him at a battered desk, a single bulb illuminating the weary expression on his face. She wondered if he wrote quickly, the words flowing uninterrupted, or whether he would stop now and then to stare into space, collecting his thoughts. Sometimes her images took one form; with the next letter they might take another, depending on what he'd written, and, Adrienne would close her eyes as she held it, trying to divine his spirit.

She wrote to him as well, answering questions that he'd asked and telling him what was going on in her life. On those days, she could almost see him beside her; if the breeze moved her hair, it was as if Paul were gently running a finger over her skin; if she heard the faint ticking of a clock, it was the sound of Pal's heart as she rested her head on his chest. But when she set the pen down, her thoughts always returned to their final moments together, holding each other on the graveled drive, the soft brush of his lips, the promise of a single year apart, then a lifetime together.

Paul also called every so often, when he had an opportunity to head into the city, and hearing the tenderness in his voice always made her heart constrict. So did the sound of his laughter or the ache in his tone as he told her how much he missed her. He called during the day, when the kids were at school, and whenever she heard the phone ringing, she found herself pausing before she answered it, hoping it was Paul. The conversations didn't last long, usually less than twenty minutes, but coupled with the letters, it was enough to get her through the next few months.

At the library, she began photocopying pages from a variety of books on Ecuador, everything from geography to history, anything that caught her eye. Once, when one of the travel magazines did a piece on the culture there, she bought the magazine and sat for hours studying the pictures and practically memorizing the article, trying to learn as much as she could about the people he was working with. Sometimes, despite herself, she wondered whether any of the women there ever looked at him with the same desire she had.

She also scanned the microfiched pages of newspapers and medical journals, looking for information on Paul's life in Raleigh. She never wrote or mentioned that she was doing this—as he often said in his letters, that was a person he never wanted to be again—but she was curious. She found the piece that had run in *The Wall Street Journal*, with a drawing of him at the top of the article. The article said he was thirty-eight, and when she stared at the face, she saw for the first time what he'd looked like when he was younger. Though she recognized his picture immediately, there were some differences that caught her eye—the darker hair parted at the side, the unlined face, the too serious, almost hard expression—that felt unfamiliar. She remembered wondering what he would think of the article now or whether he would care about it at all.

She also found some photos of him in old copies of the *Raleigh News and Observer*, meeting the governor or attending the opening of the new hospital wing at Duke Medical Center. She noted that in every picture she saw, he never seemed to smile. It was, she thought, a Paul she couldn't imagine.

In March, for no special reason, Paul arranged to have roses sent to her house and then began having them sent every month. She would place the bouquets in her room, assuming that her children would eventually notice and mention something about them; but they were lost in their own worlds and never did.

In June, she went back to Rodanthe for

a long weekend with Jean. Jean seemed edgy when she arrived, as if still trying to figure out what had upset Adrienne the last time she was there, but after an hour of easy conversation, Jean was back to normal. Adrienne walked the beach a few times that weekend, looking for another conch, but she never found one that hadn't been broken in the waves.

When she arrived back home, there was a letter from Paul with a photograph that Mark had taken. In the background was the clinic, and though Paul was thinner than he'd been six months earlier, he looked healthy. She propped the photograph against the salt and pepper shakers as she wrote him a letter in response. In his letter, he'd asked for a photograph of her, and she sorted through her photo albums until she found one that she willing to offer him.

Summer was hot and sticky; most of July was spent indoors with the air-conditioning running; in August, Matt headed off to college, while Amanda and Dan went back to high school. As the leaves on the trees turned to amber in the softer autumn sunlight, she began thinking of things that Paul and she might do together when he returned. She imagined going to the Biltmore Estate in Asheville to see the holiday decorations; she wondered what the children would think of him when he came over for Christmas dinner or what Jean would do when she booked a room at the Inn in both their names right after the New Year. No doubt, Adrienne thought with a smile, Jean would raise an eyebrow at that. Knowing her, she would say nothing at first, preferring to walk around with a smug expression that said she'd known all along and had been expecting their visit.

Now, sitting with her daughter, Adrienne recalled those plans, musing that in the past, there had been moments when she'd almost believed they'd really happened. She used to imagine the scenarios in vibrant detail, but lately she'd forced herself to stop. The regret that always followed the pleasure of these fantasies left her feeling empty, and she knew her time was better spent on those around her, who were still part of her life. She didn't want to feel the sorrow brought on by such dreams ever again. But sometimes, despite her best intentions, she simply couldn't help it.

———◆———

"Wow," Amanda murmured as she lowered the note and handed it back to her mother.

Adrienne folded it along its original crease, put it aside, then pulled out the photograph of Paul that Mark had taken.

"This is Paul," she said.

Amanda took the photo. Despite his age, he was more handsome than she had imagined. She stared at the eyes that had seemed to so captivate her mother. After a moment, she smiled.

"I can see why you fell for him. Do you have any more?"

"No," she said, "that's it."

Amanda nodded, studying the photo again.

"You described him well." She hesitated. "Did he ever send a picture of Mark?"

"No, but they look alike," Adrienne said.

"You met him?"

"Yes," she said.

"Where?"

"Here."

Amanda's eyebrows rose. "At the house?"

"He sat where you're sitting now."

"Where were we?"

"In school."

Amanda shook her head, trying to process this new information. "Your story's getting confusing," she said.

Adrienne looked away, then slowly rose from the table. As she left the kitchen, she whispered, "It was to me, too."

By October, Adrienne's father had re-covered somewhat from his earlier strokes, though not enough to allow him leave the nursing home. Adrienne had been spending time with him as always throughout the year, keeping him com-pany and doing her best to make him more comfortable.

By budgeting carefully, she'd managed to save enough to keep him in the home until April, but after that, she was at a loss as to what to do. Like the swallows to Capistrano, she always came back to this worry, though she did her best to hide her fears from him.

On most days when she arrived, the television would be blaring, as if the morning nurses believed that noise would somehow clear the fogginess in his mind. The first thing Adrienne did was turn it off. She was her father's only regular visitor besides the nurses. While she understood her children's reluctance to come, she wished they would do so anyway. Not only for her father, who wanted to see them, but for their own good as well. She had always believed it important to spend time with family in good times and in difficult ones, for the lessons it could teach.

Her father had lost the ability to speak, but she knew he could understand those who talked to him. With the right side of his face paralyzed, his smile had a crooked shape that she found endearing. It took maturity and patience to look past the exterior and see the man they had once known; though her kids had sometimes surprised her by demonstrating those qualities, they were usually uncomfortable when she'd made them visit. It was as if they looked at their grandfather and saw a future they couldn't imagine facing and were frightened by the thought that they, too, might end up that way.

She would plump his pillows before sitting beside the bed, then take his hand and talk. Most of the time she filled him in on recent events, or family, or how the children were doing, and he would stare at her, his eyes never leaving her face, silently communicating in the only way he could. Sitting beside him, she would inevitably remember her childhood—the smell of Aqua Velva on his face, pitching hay in the horse stall, the brush of stubble as he'd kissed her good night, the tender words he'd always spoken since she was a little girl.

On the day before Halloween, she went to visit him, knowing what she had to do, thinking it was time he finally knew.

"There's something I have to tell you," she began. Then, as simply as possible, she told him about Paul and how much he meant to her.

When she finished, she remembered wondering what he thought about what she'd just said. His hair was white and thinning: His eyebrows reminded her of puffs of cotton.

He smiled then, his crooked smile, and though he made no sound, when he moved his lips, she knew what he was trying to say.

The back of her throat tightened, and she leaned across the bed, resting her head on his chest. His good hand went to her back, moving weakly, soft and light. Beneath her, she could feel his ribs, brittle and frail now, and the gentle beating of his heart.

"Oh, Daddy," she whispered, "I'm proud of you, too."

———

In the living room, Adrienne went to the window and pushed aside the curtains. The street was empty, and the streetlights were circled with glowing halos. Somewhere in the distance, a dog barked a warning to a real or imagined intruder.

Amanda was still in the kitchen, though Adrienne knew she would eventually come to find her. It had been a long night for both of them, and Adrienne brought her finger to the glass.

What had they been to each other, she and Paul? Even now, she still wasn't sure. There wasn't an easy definition. He hadn't been her husband or fiancé; calling him a boyfriend made it sound as if he were a teenage infatuation; lover captured only a small part of what they had shared. He was the only person in her life, she thought, who seemed to defy description, and she wondered how many others could say the same thing about someone in their life.

Above her, a ringed moon was surrounded by indigo clouds, rolling east in the breeze. By tomorrow morning, it would be raining at the coast, and Adrienne knew she'd been right to hold back the other letters from Amanda.

What could Amanda have learned by reading them? The details of Paul's life at the clinic and how he spent his days, perhaps? Or his relationship with Mark and how it had progressed? All of that was clearly spelled out in the letters, as were his thoughts and hopes and fears, but none of that was necessary for what she hoped to impart to Amanda. The items she had set aside would be enough.

Yet once Amanda was gone, she knew she would read all of the letters again, if only because of what she'd done tonight. In the yellow light of her bedside lamp, she would run her finger over the words, savoring each one, knowing they meant more to her than anything else she owned.

Tonight, despite the presence of her daughter, Adrienne was alone. She would always be alone. She knew this as she'd told her story in the kitchen earlier, she knew this as she stood at the window now. Sometimes she wondered who she would have been had Paul never come into her life. Perhaps she would have married again, and though she suspected she would have been a good wife, she often wondered whether she would have picked a good husband.

It wouldn't have been easy. Some of her widowed or divorced friends had remarried. Most of these gentlemen they married seemed nice enough, but they were nothing like Paul. Jack, maybe, but not Paul. She believed that romance and passion were possible at any age, but she'd listened to enough of her friends to know that many relationships ended up being more trouble than they were worth. Adrienne didn't want to settle for a husband like the ones her friends had, not when she had letters reminding her of what she was missing. Would a new husband, for instance, ever whisper the words that Paul had written in his third letter, words she'd memorized the first day she'd read them?

When I sleep, I dream of you, and when I wake, I long to hold you in my arms. If anything, our time apart has only made me more certain that I want to spend my nights by your side, and my days with your heart.

Or these, from the next letter?

When I write to you, I feel your breath, when you read them, I imagine you feel mine. Is it that way with you, too? These letters are part of us now, part of our history, a reminder forever that we made it through this time. Thank you for helping me survive this year, but more than that, thank you in advance for all the years to come.

Or even these, after he and Mark had an argument later in the summer, something that inevitably left him depressed.

There's so much I wish for these days, but most of all, I wish you were here. It's strange, but before I met you, I couldn't remember the last time that I cried. Now,

*it seems that tears come easily to me . . .
but you have a way of making my sorrows
seem worthwhile, of explaining things in
a way that lessens my ache. You are a
treasure, a gift, and when we're together
again, I intend to hold you until my arms
are weak and I can do it no longer. My
thoughts of you are sometimes the only
things that keep me going.*

Staring at the distant face of the moon,
Adrienne knew the answer. No, she
thought, she wouldn't find a man like
Paul again, and as she leaned her head
against the cool pane, she sensed
Amanda's presence behind her. Adrienne
sighed, knowing it was time to finish this.

"He was going to be here for Christmas," Adrienne said, her voice so soft
that Amanda had to strain hear it. "I had
it all worked out. I'd arranged for a hotel
room," she said, "so we could be together his first night back. I even bought
a bottle of pinot grigio." She paused.

"There's a letter from Mark in the box on the table that explains everything."

"What happened?"

In the darkness, Adrienne finally turned. Her face was half in shadow, and at the expression on her mother's face, Amanda felt a sudden chill.

It took a moment for Adrienne to answer, the words floating through the darkness.

"Don't you know?" she whispered.

Seventeen

The letter, Amanda saw, had been written on the same notebook paper that Paul had used to write the note. Noticing that her hands were trembling slightly, Amanda laid them flat on the table.

Then, with a deep breath, she lowered her gaze.

Dear Adrienne,

As I sit here, I realize that I don't even know how I'm supposed to begin a letter like this. After all, we've never met, and though I know of you through my father, it's not the same. Part of me wishes I was able to do this in person, but due to my injuries, I couldn't leave just yet. So here I am, struggling for words, and wondering if anything I write will mean anything at all.

I'm sorry that I didn't call, but then, I decided that it wasn't going to be any easier to hear what I have to say. I'm still trying to make sense of it myself, and that's part of the reason I'm writing.

I know my father told you about me, but I think it's important that you know our history from my perspective. My hope is that it'll give you a good idea of the man who loved you.

You have to understand that when I was growing up, I didn't have a father. Yes, he lived in the house; yes, he provided for my mom and me; but he was never around, unless it was to reprimand me about the B I'd received on a report card. I remember that when I was a kid, my school had a science fair that I participated in every year, and from kindergarten through eighth grade, my father never made it once. He never took me to a baseball game, or played catch in the yard, or even went with me on a bike ride. He mentioned that he'd told you some of this, but believe me when I tell you that it was worse than he probably made it seem. When I left for Ecuador, I honestly remember hoping that I'd never see him again.

Then, of all things, he decided to come here, to be with me. You have to understand that deep down, there'd always been an arrogance about my father that I'd grown to detest, and I figured he was coming down because of that. I could imagine him suddenly trying to act like a father, dishing out advice that I didn't need or want. Or reorganizing the clinic to make it more efficient, or coming up with brilliant ideas to make the place more livable for us. Or even calling in some debts owed to him over the years to bring a whole crew of young volunteer physicians to work at the clinic, all the while making sure the entire press corps back home knew exactly who was responsible for all the good deeds. My father had always loved to see his name in print, and he was acutely aware of what good publicity could do for him and his practice. By the time he arrived, I was actually thinking of packing my bags and going home, leaving him behind. I had a dozen responses lined up for just about anything I thought he might say. Apology? A little late for that. Good to see you? Wish 1 could say the same. I think we should talk? I don't think that would be a good idea. Instead, all he said was, "Hey," and when he saw my expression, he simply nodded and walked away. That was our only contact during the first week he was there.

It didn't get much better right away. For months, I kept expecting him to revert to his old ways, and I watched for it, ready to call him on it. But he never did. He never complained about the work or the conditions, he offered suggestions only when asked directly, and though he never took credit for it, the director finally admitted that my father had been the one who supplied the new medicines and equipment we'd desperately needed, though he'd insisted that his gift remain anonymous.

What I think I most appreciated was that he didn't pretend we were something we weren't. For months, we weren't friends and I didn't regard him as a father, yet he never tried to change my mind about those things. He didn't pressure me in any way, and I think that's when I began to let my guard down about him.

I guess what I'm trying to say is that my father had changed, and little by little, I began to think there was something about him that was worth a second chance. And though I know he'd made some changes before he met you, you were the main reason he became the person he did. Before he met you, he was trying to find something. After you came along, he'd already found it.

My father talked about you all the time,

and I can only imagine how many letters he must have sent you. He loved you, but I'm sure you know that. What you might not know is that before you came along, I'm not entirely convinced that he knew what loving someone meant. My father had accomplished a lot of things in his life, but I'm certain he would have traded it all for a lifetime with you instead. Considering he was married to my mother, it isn't easy for me to write this, but I thought you'd want to know. And part of me knows that he would be pleased at the thought that I understood how much you meant to him.

Somehow, you changed my father, and because of you, I wouldn't trade this last year for anything. I don't know how you did it, but you made my father into a man that I miss already. You saved him, and by doing so, I guess that in a way, you saved me as well.

He was at the outreach clinic in the mountains because of me, you know. It was absolutely terrible that night. It had been raining for days, roads everywhere washing out in the mud. When I radioed the main clinic to say that I couldn't make it back because my Jeep wouldn't start, and that a major mudslide was imminent, he was the one who commandeered another Jeep—over the director's frantic protests—to try to reach me. My dad came to save me, and when I saw it was him sitting behind the wheel, I think it was the first time I'd ever thought of him in that way. Until that point, he'd always been my father, but not my dad, if you know what I mean.

We made it out just in time. Within minutes, we heard the roar as the side of the mountain gave way, destroying the clinic instantly, and I remember that we glanced at each other then, unable to believe how close it had been.

I wish I could tell you what went wrong after that, but I can't. He was driving carefully and we'd almost made it back. I could even see the lights from the clinic in the valley below. But suddenly, the Jeep started to skid as we rounded a sharp curve, and the next thing I knew, we were off the road and tumbling down the mountain.

Other than breaking my arm and several ribs, I was okay, but I knew immediately that my dad wasn't. I remember screaming at him to hold on, that I'd go get help, but he grabbed my hand and held me in place. I think even he knew it was almost over, and he wanted me to stay with him.

Then, this man who had just saved my life, asked me to forgive him.

He loved you, Adrienne. Please don't ever forget that. Despite the short time you spent with him, he adored you, and I'm terribly sorry for your loss. When things are hard, as they are for me, fall back on the knowledge that not only would he have done the same thing for you that he did for me, but because of you, I was given the chance to get to know, and love, my dad.

I guess what I'm trying to say is, thank you.

                                        Mark Flanner

Amanda lowered the letter to the table. It was almost dark in the kitchen now, and she could hear the sound of her own breath. Her mother had stayed in the living room, alone with her thoughts, and Amanda folded the letter, thinking of Paul now, thinking of her mother, and, oddly, thinking of Brent.

With effort, she could recall that Christmas so many years ago—how quiet her mother had been, the smiles that always seemed a little forced, the unexplained tears that they'd all assumed had something to do with their father.

And, through it all, she had said nothing.

Despite the fact her mother and Paul hadn't had the years together that she'd had with Brent, Amanda knew with sudden certainty that Paul's death had struck her mother with the same intensity that Amanda experienced when sitting beside Brent's bed for the very last time—with one difference.

Unlike her, her mother hadn't been given the chance to say good-bye.

When she heard the muted sounds of her daughter's sobs, Adrienne turned from the window in the living room and made her way to the kitchen. Amanda looked up in silence, her eyes filled with unspoken anguish.

Adrienne stood without moving, watching her daughter, then finally opened her arms. Instinctively Amanda rose, trying and failing to stop her tears, and mother and daughter stood in the kitchen, holding each other for a long, long time.

Eighteen

—◆—

The air had chilled slightly, and Adrienne had lit a few candles around the kitchen to warm and light the space. Sitting at the table, she had put Mark's letter back in the box with the note and the photograph. Amanda watched her soberly, her hands in her lap.

"I'm sorry, Mom," she said quietly. "For everything. For losing Paul, for having to live through that alone. I can't imagine what it must have been like to keep all of that inside."

"Neither can I," Adrienne said. "There's no way I could have made it without help."

Amanda shook her head. "But you did," she whispered.

"No," Adrienne said. "I survived, but I didn't do it alone."

Amanda looked puzzled. Adrienne offered her a melancholy smile.

"Grampa," she finally said. "My daddy. That's who I cried with. And I cried with him every day for weeks. Without him, I don't know what I would have done."

"But . . ." Amanda trailed off, and Adrienne went on for her.

"But he couldn't say anything?" Adrienne paused. "He didn't have to. He listened, and that was what I needed. Besides, I knew there wasn't anything he could have said that would have made the pain go away, even if he could speak." She lifted her gaze. "You know that as well as I do."

Amanda pressed her lips together. "I wish you'd told me," she said. "Before now, I mean."

"Because of Brent?"

Amanda nodded.

"I know you do, but you weren't ready to hear it until now. You needed time to work through your grief in your own way, on your own terms."

For a long moment, Amanda said nothing.

"It isn't fair. You and Paul, me and Brent," she whispered.

"No, it isn't."

"How were you able to go on after losing him like that?"

Adrienne smiled wistfully. "I took things one day at a time. Isn't that what they tell you to do? I know it sounds trite, but I used to wake up in the mornings and tell myself that I only had to be strong for one day. Just one day. I did that over and over."

"You make it sound so simple," Amanda whispered.

"It wasn't. It was the hardest time I ever went through."

"Even more than when Daddy left?"

"That was hard, too, but this was different." Adrienne flashed a quick smile. "You were the one who told me that, remember?"

Amanda looked away. Yes, she thought, I do. "I wish I'd had the chance to meet him."

"You would have liked him. In time, I mean. Back then, you might not have. You were still hoping that your dad and I would get back together."

Amanda's hand went reflexively to the wedding band she still wore, and she spun it around her finger, her face a mask.

"You've lost a lot in your life."

"Yes, I have."

"But you seem so happy now."

"I am."

"How can you be?"

Adrienne brought her hands together. "When I think of losing Paul or the years that might have been, of course it makes me sad. It did then, and it still does now. But you have to understand something else, too: As hard as it was, as terrible and unfair as the way things turned out, I wouldn't have traded the few days I spent with him for anything."

She paused, making sure her daughter understood that. "In Mark's letter, he said that I saved Paul from himself. But if Mark had asked me, I would have said that we'd saved each other, or that he'd saved me. Had I never met him, I doubt I ever would have forgiven Jack, and I wouldn't have been the mother or grandmother I am now. Because of him, I came back to Rocky Mount knowing that I was going to be okay, that things would work out, that no matter what, I'd make it. And the year we spent writing each other gave me the strength I needed when I finally learned what had happened to him. Yes, I was devastated by losing him, but if somehow I could go back in time—this time knowing what would happen in advance—I still would have wanted him to go because of his son. He needed to make things right with Mark. His son needed him—had always needed him. And it wasn't too late."

Amanda looked away, knowing she was talking about Max and Greg as well.

"That's why I told you this story from the beginning," Adrienne went on. "Not just because I'd been through what you're living through now, but because I wanted you to understand how important his relationship with his son was. And what it meant for Mark to know that. Those are wounds that are difficult to heal, and I don't want you to have any more wounds than you already have now."

Adrienne reached across the table and took her daughter's hand. "I know you're still hurting about Brent, and there's nothing I can do to help you with that. But if Brent were here, he would tell you to concentrate on your kids, not on his death. He would want you to remember the good moments, not the bad ones. And above all, he would want to know that you're going to be okay, too."

"I know all that—"

Adrienne cut her off with a gentle squeeze, not letting her finish. "You're stronger than you think you are," she went on, "but only if you want to be."

"It's not that easy."

"Of course it isn't, but you have to understand that I'm not talking about your emotions. Those you can't control. You're still going to cry, you're still going to have moments when you don't feel you can go on. But you have to act as if you can. At a time like this, actions are just about the only things you *can* control." She paused. "Your children need you, Amanda. I don't think there's ever been a time when they needed you more. But lately, you haven't been there for them. I know you're hurting, and I hurt for you, but you're a mom now, and you can't keep going like this. Brent wouldn't have wanted it, and your children are paying the price."

As Adrienne finished, Amanda seemed to be studying the table. But then, almost as if moving in slow motion, she raised her head and looked up.

As much as she wished otherwise, Adrienne had no idea what Amanda was thinking.

***

Dan was folding the last of the towels in the basket while watching ESPN when Amanda returned home. The clothes had been sorted into piles on the coffee table. Dan automatically reached for the remote to turn down the volume.

"I was wondering when you were going to make it back," he said.

"Oh, hey," Amanda said, looking around. "Where are the boys?"

Dan motioned with his head as he added a green towel to the stack. "They just got into bed a few minutes ago. They're probably still awake if you want to say good night."

"Where are your kids?"

"I dropped them off with Kira on our

way home. Just to let you know, Max dripped some pizza sauce on his Scooby-Doo shirt. I guess it's one of his favorites, because he got pretty upset about it. I've got it soaking in the sink now, but I couldn't find the stain remover."

Amanda nodded. "I'll get some this weekend. I've got to go shopping anyway. I'm out of other things, too."

Dan looked at his sister. "If you make a list, Kira could pick up what you need. I know she's going to the store."

"Thanks for the offer, but it's time I start doing that for myself again."

"Okay . . ." He smiled uncertainly. For a moment, neither he nor his sister said anything.

"Thanks for taking the boys out," Amanda said finally.

Dan shrugged. "No big deal. We were going out anyway, and I figured they might enjoy it."

Amanda's voice was earnest. "No. I mean, thank you for all the times you've done that lately. Not just tonight. You and Matt have been great since . . . since I lost Brent, and I don't know if I've let you know how much I appreciate that."

Dan looked away at the mention of Brent's name. He reached for the empty laundry basket.

"What are uncles for, right?" He shifted from one foot to the other, holding the basket in front of him. "Would you like me to swing by for the boys again tomorrow? I was thinking of going on a bike ride with the kids."

Amanda shook her head. "Thanks, but I think I'll pass."

Dan looked at her, his expression dubious. Amanda didn't seem to notice. She slipped off her jacket and set it on the chair along with her purse. "I talked to Mom for quite a while tonight."

"Oh? How'd it go?"

"You wouldn't believe half of it if I told you."

"What did she say?"

"You had to be there. But I learned something about her tonight."

Dan cocked an eyebrow, waiting.

"She's tougher than she looks," Amanda said.

Dan laughed. "Yeah . . . sure, she's tough all right. She cries when the goldfish die."

"That may be true, but in a lot of ways, I wish I could be as strong as she is."

"I'll bet."

When Dan saw his sister's serious expression, he suddenly realized no punch line was coming. His brow furrowed.

"Wait," he said. "*Our* mom?"

<hr/>

Dan left a few minutes later, and despite his attempts to find out what their mother had told Amanda, she had refused to tell him. She understood the reasons for her mother's silence, both in the past and in the years since, and knew her mother would tell Dan when or if she had reason to do so.

Amanda locked the door behind Dan

and looked around the living room. In addition to folding the clothes, he'd straightened up; she remembered that before she'd left, there were videos strewn near the television, a pile of empty cups on the end table, a year's worth of magazines stacked haphazardly on the desk by the door.

Dan had taken care of everything. Again.

Amanda turned out the lights, thinking of Brent, thinking of the last eight months, thinking of her children. Greg and Max shared a bedroom at one end of the hall; the master bedroom was at the opposite end. Lately the distance had seemed too far to travel at the end of the day. Before Brent had passed away, she'd helped the boys say their prayers and read to them from small books with colorful drawings before pulling up the covers to their chins.

Tonight, her brother had done that for her. Last night, no one had done it at all.

Amanda headed upstairs. The house

was dark, the upper hallway shadowed and black. At the top of the steps, she heard the broken whispers of her sons. She went down the corridor and paused in the doorway of their room, peeking in.

They slept in twin beds, their comforters decorated with dinosaurs and race cars; toys were scattered between the beds. A night-light glowed from the outlet near the closet, and in the silence, she saw again how much both boys resembled their father.

They'd stopped moving. Knowing she was watching them, they wanted her to think they were asleep, as if finding security by hiding from their mother.

The floor squeaked beneath her weight. Max seemed to be holding his breath. Greg peeked at her, then snapped his eyelids shut as Amanda sat beside him. Leaning over, she kissed him on the cheek and ran a gentle hand through his hair.

"Hey," she whispered. "Are you sleeping?"

"Yes," he said.

Amanda smiled. "Do you want to sleep with Mommy tonight? In the big bed?" she whispered.

It seemed to take a moment before Greg understood what she'd said. "With you?"

"Yeah."

"Okay," he said, and Amanda kissed him again, watching as he sat up. She moved to Max's bed. His hair glittered gold in the light from the window, looking like Christmas tinsel.

"Hey, sweetie."

Max swallowed, his eyes closed. "Can I come, too?"

"If you want to."

"Okay," he said.

Amanda smiled as they got up, but when they started toward the door, Amanda pulled them back, embracing them both. They smelled like little boys: dirt and sweet grass, innocence itself.

"How about if tomorrow we go to the

park, and later we can get some ice cream," she said.

"Can we fly our kites?" Max asked.

Amanda squeezed them tighter, closing her eyes.

"All day long. And the next day, too, if you want to."

Nineteen

❦

It was past midnight now, and in her room, Adrienne held the conch as she sat on the bed. Dan had called an hour earlier, full of news about Amanda.

"She told me she was going to take the boys out tomorrow, just the three of them. That they needed to spend some time with their mom." He paused. "I don't know what you said, but I guess whatever it was worked."

"I'm glad."

"So what did you say to her? She was, you know, kind of circumspect about it."

"The same thing I've been saying all

along. The same thing you and Matt have been saying."

"Then why did she listen to you this time?"

"I guess," Adrienne said, drawing out the words, "because she finally wanted to."

Later, after she'd hung up the phone, Adrienne read the letters from Paul, just as she'd known she would. Though his words were hard to see through her tears, her own words were even harder to read. She'd read those countless times, too, the ones she had written to Paul in the year they'd been apart. Her own letters had been in the second stack, the stack that Mark Flanner had brought with him when he'd come to her house two months after Paul had been buried in Ecuador.

Amanda had forgotten to ask about Mark's visit before she'd gone, and Adrienne hadn't reminded her. In time, Amanda might bring it up again, but even now, Adrienne wasn't sure how much she would say. This was the one part of the story she'd kept entirely to herself over the years, locked away, like the letters. Even her father didn't know what Paul had done.

In the pale glow of the streetlight shining through her window, Adrienne rose from the bed and took a jacket and scarf from the closet, then walked downstairs. She unlocked the back door and stepped outside.

Stars were blazing like tiny sparkles on a magician's cape, and the air was moist and cold. In the yard, she could see blackened pools, reflecting the ebony above. Lights shone from neighbors' windows, and though she knew it was just her imagination, she could almost smell salt in the air, as if sea mist were rolling over the neighborhood yards.

Mark had come to the house on a February morning; his arm was still in a sling, but she'd barely noticed it. Instead, she found herself staring at him, unable to turn away. He looked, she thought, exactly like his father. When he offered the saddest of smiles as she opened the door, Adrienne took a small step backward, trying hard to hold back the tears.

They sat at the table, two coffee cups between them, and Mark removed the letters from the bag he'd brought with him.

"He saved them," he said. "I didn't know what else to do with them, except to bring them to you."

Adrienne nodded as she took them.

"Thank you for your letter," she said. "I know how hard it must have been for you to write it."

"You're welcome," he said, and for a long time, he was silent. Then, of course, he told her why he'd come.

Now, on the porch, Adrienne smiled as she thought about what Paul had done for her. She remembered going to visit her father in the nursing home after Mark had left, the place her father would never have to leave. As Mark had explained as he'd sat at the table, Paul had already made arrangements for her father to be taken care of there until the end of his days—a gift he had hoped to surprise her with. When she began to protest, Mark made it clear that it would have broken his heart to know that she wouldn't accept it.

"Please," he finally said, "it's what my dad wanted."

In the years that followed, she would cherish Paul's final gesture, just as she cherished every memory of the few days they spent together. Paul still meant everything to her, would always mean everything to her, and in the chilly air of a late winter evening, Adrienne knew she would always feel that way.

She'd already lived through more years than she had remaining, but it hadn't seemed that long. Entire years had slipped from her memory, washed away like sandy footprints near the water's edge. With the exception of the time she'd spent with Paul Flanner, she sometimes believed that she had passed through life with no more awareness than that of a small child on a long car ride, staring out the window as the scenery rolled past.

She had fallen in love with a stranger in the course of a weekend, and she would never fall in love again. The desire to love again had ended on a mountain pass in Ecuador. Paul had died for his son, and in that moment, part of her had died as well.

She wasn't bitter, though. In the same situation, she knew she would have tried to save her own child as well. Yes, Paul was gone, but he had left her with so much. She'd found love and joy, she'd found a strength she never knew she had, and nothing could ever take those things away.

But all of it was over now, all except the memories, and she'd constructed those with infinite care. They were as real to her as the scene she was staring at now, and blinking back the tears that had started falling in the empty darkness of her bedroom, she raised her chin. Staring into the sky, she breathed deeply, listening to the distant and imagined echo of waves as they broke along the shore on a stormy night in Rodanthe.